Regenerate

Wendy Cartmell

Costa Press

Copyright © Wendy Cartmell 2014
Published by Costa Press
2nd Edition 2015
ISBN 13: 978-1494981112
ISBN 10: 1494981114
Wendy Cartmell has asserted her right under the Copyright Designs and Patents Act 1998 to be identified as the author of this work.
All characters and events in this publication, other than those in the public domain, are fictitious and any resemblance to real persons, living or dead is purely coincidental.

re-gen-er-ate

1. To form, construct, or create anew, especially in an improved state.
2. To give new life or energy to; revitalize.

Death

"Did you know it's been three months since you died and three months since our daughter was born?" Kerry asked Alan, although in truth he wasn't in the room. "I suppose you could say it's our anniversary - of sorts.

"Death tends to be the main reason Army wives get a visit from the military police," she told him, "so when I saw two of them walking up the path to our house, dressed in their sober black suits and dark coats, I knew the reason for their visit before they had the chance to knock. I went into labour right there on the front doorstep. Must have been the shock. God knows what the RMP must have thought. They'd come to tell me you'd been killed in Afghanistan and would have been expecting tears. Instead they got broken waters, labour pains and screams. Still, a soldier has to cope with all types of situations, so they dealt with me the best they could until an ambulance came and took me away."

Kerry laughed and said, "That makes me think of that song, 'they're coming to take me away, ha ha,'" and she began singing, giving Alan a rendition of the song, which was nothing like the writer of the piece envisaged.

Sobering up, she then said, "One of these days someone might just do that, you know. Take me away. But it won't be the Army who do it. Oh no. I'm persona non grata now with that lot. Since you died, that is."

Kerry twisted a curl of ginger hair around her finger and hoped that if she stared at the empty armchair long enough and hard enough, she'd be able to see Alan. She'd sensed in him the flat for a while now, but never seen him. At least he hadn't abandoned her altogether, she reasoned, so she continued talking to him.

"They had the decency to wait until after the funeral before they told me they were chucking me out of our Army house. Army policy or some such thing. It seems that once a husband dies the wife left behind is not their responsibility. Nothing to do with them. So they hid behind their regulations. It was in my best interests for them to serve me with an eviction order, they said. That way the council could re-house me, they said. The council would find a nice place for me and my daughter, they said."

She was still addressing the chair she felt sure Alan was sitting in.

"So I'm out of their hair now. Off Aldershot Garrison and stuck in this dump in North Camp, a small village in between Aldershot and Farnborough. You remember North Camp don't you?" she asked him. "You know, where that café is. The one everyone goes to for a cheap meal. Well I'm there, in a pokey apartment which has mould on the walls and a boiler that has a worse cough than I do. Come on let me give you a tour," she said and jumped off the settee. As she did so, she revealed tears in the fabric that had been concealed beneath the large green jumper she wore over a pair of black leggings.

Kerry wandered around the room, showing Alan points of interest, including the damp patch that was marching down the wall, chasing away the wallpaper, which was forming the shape of a curling wave as it peeled off.

"Look, Alan, I cleaned the kitchen," she said as she continued the tour. "It took me all day mind and I used a whole bottle of bleach," she told him proudly as she walked the few steps to the kitchen door, inclining her head as she listened to his response. "I know the doors on the cabinets don't fit properly and there's a leaky tap," she said. "So what if the flooring is ripped in places with big chunks missing? At least it's bloody clean!" Kerry ended up shouting the last sentence and had to take a moment to reign in her temper.

She returned to the settee and stared at his chair.

"Sorry, I didn't mean to shout. It's just that I've been under a bit of pressure lately. Missing you, you know?"

She shrugged her slender shoulders, making her curls bounce.

"It's just - oh I don't know - you were such a good bloke, Alan. I know people always say that when someone has died. They don't want to admit the deceased had any faults. Don't speak ill of the dead and all that. But you really were a good husband and soldier. You would have made a good father too, if you'd been given the chance. But you weren't."

Kerry started rocking backwards and forwards, her arms wrapped around her slight body.

"So instead we're both rotting away. You in your grave and me in this flat."

Suddenly she lifted her head.

"Oh, I forgot. You never did see our daughter, Molly, did you? She doesn't look much like you - or me, come to that. She just looks like a baby. She doesn't have my long nose, hers is a small button one and she doesn't have my high cheekbones, hers are all full and pink and shiny as apples. She's not even got our hair. Yours was dark and mine is ginger. Hey, maybe that's why she's turned out to have blond hair. My green eyes and your brown ones have become her blue ones and she has lovely thick lashes which looks so cute when her eyes are closed.

"That reminds me, she hasn't woken up for her last feed of the day. I better go and see if she's alright. She might just be lying there quietly, looking at her mobile. She does that sometimes. Gets captivated with something and spends ages fascinated by it. Come on," she said standing up. "Her cot is in my bedroom. Well, the only bedroom actually. I just managed to squeeze it in by having a single bed for me instead of a double one. Well, I don't need a double bed anymore do I? Single, that's me. Widowed at 26. Who'd have thought it?" she called to him as she walked to the bedroom.

"See, Alan, there she is, our lovely Molly," Kerry said stopping by the cot. "She's the only thing I have left of you. Well apart from your uniform, medals and dog tags."

Her hand fingered the dog tags she wore around her neck, suspended on a silver chain.

"Oh and the flag your coffin was draped in. Mustn't forget that," and she looked at the flag that she'd placed on the dressing table beneath his photograph. It was still folded as neatly as when she'd been handed it by Alan's friend from his unit after the funeral.

"Oh how sweet, look, Molly's clutching her little

blanket. It's her favourite. It was hanging over the cot railings. She must have pulled it off. Why is it all over her face? She won't be able to breathe. Silly Molly, I best take it off her," Kerry said as she leaned into the cot, removing the blanket covering her daughter's face and placing it on her own bed.

Turning back to the cot, she looked more closely at Molly.

"That's strange, her lips are blue." Reaching out for the baby and touching her arm, she said, "She feels cold to the touch as well. Maybe if I wrap her in her blanket, I can warm her up and then she'll be okay. What do you think, Alan?"

Kerry quickly grabbed the blanket and spread it out on the bed. Placing the immobile baby on it, she wrapped it around Molly and scooped her up.

Rocking the child gently in her arms she said, "Come on, Molly, breathe. Perhaps if mummy rubs your back and arms that might help to get your circulation going."

She placed Molly on the single bed on her back and rubbed the baby's cold limbs. Molly wasn't the only one having trouble breathing. So was Kerry. She was holding her breath in fear and then realising what she was doing, gulped in a large breath of air.

When rubbing Molly to get her circulation going didn't work, Kerry said, "How about if I pinch your nose and blow into your mouth. Or push on your little chest to get your heart beating again. Alan!" she screamed in panic as she once more picked up Molly, oblivious to her tears, which were wetting the baby's head. "Nothing's working… she's not responding… I don't know what else to do. I think I'll just climb into bed with her and maybe my body will warm her up… it works for people with hypothermia… perhaps that's what's wrong with her. It can be pretty cold in this flat. Yes, I think that's best. Come on, Molly, let's get into bed."

Kerry pulled back the lumpy duvet and climbed into the small bed. Lying down and pulling it over them both, she whispered, "Mummy will make you feel better, Molly. I promise."

1

The baby was waiting for them when they arrived at the Royal Garrison Church. It was tucked into a corner by the north entrance door. Wrapped in a pink woollen blanket. One minute, the Padre of the church, Captain Francis Symmonds and his newly married wife, Kim, an ex-Sgt in the RMP, were strolling along, arm in arm in the bright sunshine; the next, they were confronted by what appeared to be an abandoned dead baby. The shock was profound. They stopped just inside the brick built vestibule and stone archway that protected the old oak door and offered shelter from the elements. There was an eerie stillness. There was no noise from inside the church and the sounds of the road beyond the north entrance were muted, hushed by the thickness of the stone and brick that surrounded them. The bundle was placed by the large, solid door, pushed up against the stone portico. All they could see was a small round face with a tuft of blond hair poking out of the blanket that covered not only the little body, but also the head. It reminded Francis of a mummified Egyptian baby.

They looked at the baby and then at each other.

"Do you think…?"

Kim couldn't seem to finish the sentence so Francis did it for her, "…it's dead? Yes, I think it's safe to assume that. Look, the child's not moving. There's no shuffling, murmuring or crying."

Kim rubbed at her eyes brushing away her tears and turned her head away from the pitiful sight, but Francis felt compelled to reach out and pick up the child.

"Stop!" Kim called, as he moved towards the child. "Don't touch it. We should treat this as a crime scene."

"Crime scene?" he said, quickly retrieving his hands and stuffing them in his uniform trouser pockets, to keep them out of the way. They were itching to pick up the baby and... what? He wasn't sure, he just had this need to hold the child in his arms and offer it some kind of comfort, he supposed. "Isn't it just a case of a poor child that has died being left at the church door?" he asked her.

"We don't know that," Kim answered, "and we won't do until after the post mortem. Until then we should treat this as a crime scene. I'd better call in it."

Kim busied herself with ringing firstly DI Anderson of the local Aldershot Police and then Sgt Major Crane from the Special Investigations Branch of the Military Police, Kim's ex-boss. Both men needed to know about the child: the Aldershot Police because the baby was a civilian and the SIB as it was abandoned on a military garrison.

Francis watched Kim at work. She was dressed in civvies, rather than her Army uniform. It still felt strange, not seeing her in her uniform any more. While they were 'going out' they'd both been in the Army and therefore more often than not in uniform. As she'd now left the forces, she was permanently in civvies. At first she'd swapped her khaki uniform for black trousers worn with tailored shirts. But as she seemed to relax into her new life and her new role as the wife of the Padre, her dress had become more informal, which more often than not meant she wore jeans. Which was fine by him. She looked bloody good in jeans.

Today she was wearing what he believed the fashionistas called skinny jeans, which clung to her long legs, emphasising their length and ankle boots. She had teamed those with a red jumper and blue tailored jacket. Her blond hair was scraped back into a pony tail and she had a light touch of colour on her cheeks.

He was being introduced to a whole new world by Kim. The world of women. He learned how some women had a fixation with their clothes, make-up and hair, as he read with interest his wife's magazines. Let's face it, during his formative years he had been more concerned with God than girls. But he only read them when she wasn't there, of course. He thought of it as gathering background information. She would have found it hilarious. So he kept it quiet, a kind of guilty secret.

Bringing his thoughts back to the present situation, he reflected on who would do such a thing? Leave a dead baby at the church? Whoever it was needed help. He considered a range of scenarios. A young girl who had given birth in secret? A woman caught unawares, whose child was still-born? A baby that had died in the night and the parents didn't know what to do?

Still watching Kim, he couldn't imagine the unspeakable horror of losing so young a child, for from what he had seen, it looked new born, or at the most only a couple of months old. How would he and Kim feel if it was their child that had died? Not that they had any children. Not yet at any rate. That was something that he was looking forward to. But it would be sometime in their future probably, for that was a conversation they hadn't had as yet.

He then thought about the different ways the baby could have died. Cot death, naturally, or shaking the child, unnaturally. It, for Francis didn't yet know if it was a boy or a girl, could have died from heart failure, lung failure or a myriad of other natural causes. But the thing most concerning the Padre at that moment was the parents. He figured that someone must be pretty desperate to leave a dead child at God's door. Still keeping some way away from the baby, as instructed, he made the sign of the cross in its direction and then prayed for the child's soul and for the souls of its parents.

Sgt Major Crane was the first to arrive on the scene as a result of Kim's phone calls and he came to stand next to the Padre. After finishing his silent prayers the Padre raised his head. "Morning, Crane. Good to see you," he said and shook the investigator's hand. "Sorry we're meeting under such circumstances. It seems to be the nature of our meetings these days."

"Yes, sir, I'm afraid it does. What a bloody awful thing."

"Do you mean the death of the child or the leaving of it at the church?"

"Both, Padre, both," and Francis watched Crane worry at the short dark beard he'd been given permission to grow and which hid the disfiguring scar that ran from his ear to his chin. "Excuse me, sir," Crane went on, "but I see Major Martin has arrived."

As the investigator moved away, Francis was confident that if anyone could find out who the parents of the child were, it would be Sgt Major Tom Crane. He had great faith in the man, after working with him on a several occasions and had nothing but admiration for the results he obtained. Alright, there were those who said he was unconventional, insubordinate and without doubt a huge pain in the arse to work with. But Francis had come to realise that those were excellent qualities for an Army investigator.

He watched Crane and Kim talk to the retired Major, who was now a pathologist at the nearby Frimley Park Hospital. They were quickly joined by Sgt Billy Williams, also from the SIB, who had arrived with his forensic kit and by DI Anderson. They recounted what had happened so far. Or rather what had not happened, as they'd all been careful to stay away from the baby and the church door.

The Major and Billy bundled themselves up in crime scene suits, pulling on overshoes and putting up the hoods over their hair. The Major waddled to the church door, encumbered by his suit and his case, looking a bit like the Michelin Man. Well, a lot, actually. Francis thought that Billy being younger, taller and broader around the chest than the Major, wore his suit with rather more panache.

"Sorry, Francis, I've been ignoring you," Kim said as she walked over to him.

He put his arm around her shoulders, "Of course you haven't. I'm just glad you were here to deal with it so competently."

"Thanks, it's, um, been a step back in time, I guess."

"Well, you've not forgotten what to do," he joked. "You kept me in check at any rate," and he smiled down at her.

She gave him a small smile in return but Francs glimpsed sadness in Kim's eyes. She looked away from him, her blond pony tail swishing, as though she wanted to end the conversation. But he pressed on.

"And how do you feel about falling back into an RMP role?"

He couldn't help it, he had to ask her. He'd always been concerned that once Kim was over her pneumonia and back to full health, she might regret her decision to leave the Royal Military Police in order to marry him. Military rules stated that a serving soldier couldn't marry anyone of a higher rank and stay in the Army. So instead of being a busy and respected office manager within the Branch, she was now just a vicar's wife.

"Is that what's troubling you?" he asked her. "Because something is. And has been for a while."

"No, Francis, I'm fine," she replied.

But he knew she wasn't, as he watched her walk away from him and return to DI Anderson and Crane.

Molly

Kerry banged her way into the flat, jostling the pram through the door and pushing it into the sitting room. She paused for a moment after closing the apartment door, leaning back against it, trying to calm down and still her shaking hands.

"I'm back now, Alan," she said. "I'm still a bit wobbly, mind you, so I think I'll lie down on the bed for a minute." She pushed herself off the door and then remembered. "No. No, I won't do that, the settee will do for now. I can't face Molly's cot just yet. Molly's empty cot. I couldn't keep my promise, Alan. Couldn't make Molly better. Sorry," she sniffed. "Just let me pull myself together and mop up these tears, and then I can tell you what happened. I want to write it down in my diary afterwards as well and I don't want the pages to get wet and be a permanent reminder of my sorrow."

Kerry took her coat off, threw it on the settee and fumbled in her trouser pockets. She pulled out a balled up tissue and wiped her eyes. Plopping on the sofa, she started to pick it apart as she talked. "Right that's better," she took a deep breath. "So," she exhaled, "when I woke up this morning, Molly was still cold. She wasn't breathing and her pretty face was like porcelain. Drained of blood. Drained of life. She looked just like a doll, lying there, not moving.

"I picked her up and could smell her nappy needed changing. It was very hard to put the new one on. Her little legs and arms were rigid, though I managed it in the end. I didn't want her to be left in a dirty nappy. I tried to dress her in her best clothes, but that was impossible and I didn't want to hurt her by forcing her legs and arms into positions they just didn't want to go. The next best thing I could think of was to wrap her in her favourite blanket. So that's what I did and placed her in her pram, pulling up the hood and popping the cover into place." Kerry wiped her damp hands against her black trousers and took her cardigan off, throwing it on top of her coat.

"We walked out of the flat as though nothing was wrong. Just another day for Molly and me. Taking a walk in the sunshine. The lift smelled disgusting as usual. As you know, the only way I can use it is by taking a deep breath before I get in and then holding my breath as long as I can, as the lift creaks and groans its way to the ground floor. I'm glad Molly didn't smell that stench. Didn't pull that fetid air into her clean lungs."

Kerry paused in her retelling and tipped her head on one side, listening.

"Where did we go? That's what I was just about to tell you, if you'll stop interrupting. Anyway, as we walked along the road I knew I had to decide where to go. I needed a safe place. A place where Molly would be looked after. I considered the hospital, but was wary of the CCTV cameras that are everywhere these days. I naturally gravitated towards Aldershot Garrison, the place I really consider my home. It was quite a walk, but I didn't mind. Molly and I didn't have anything better to do.

"Walking through the Garrison I was racking my brains, trying to think of where to go. I considered your Barracks, but then remembered the Regiment was still in Afghanistan, so that was no good and that's when I saw the best place for Molly. The Royal Garrison Church. Do you remember it? It was the one we got married in and the one where your funeral service was held. I remembered the Padre, Captain Symmonds I think his name is. Such a lovely man. And his wife is nice as well. Kath? Kathy? Oh, yes, I've got it now. Kim. Kim Symmonds. I was sure she'd understand and help Molly. Keep her safe. Make sure she went to Heaven, to meet you." Kerry looked down and as she had shredded the tissue, she brushed the bits onto the floor and started to pick at the studs pressed into her tee-shirt instead.

"I took Molly out of her pram, made sure she was tightly swathed in her blanket and left her by the church door," she continued. "I walked away on legs that were bound in elastic, tying me to Molly. But I knew I had to resist their pull and bit by bit I managed to break away. Snapped each tendril, one by one. But my heart wasn't as lucky. I felt it tear out of my body and fly to my baby. So I left that behind, as well as my daughter.

"I expect you think I'm a bit strange, leaving Molly at the church like that. Not telling anyone. Not making arrangements for her myself. But, you see, if I admit to anyone that our baby has died, they'll chuck me out of this flat. I won't be a single mother entitled to housing anymore. I know this place is the pits, but they'll throw me out onto the street. And I hope you understand that

I just can't cope with that, Alan. Not at the minute. I can't risk losing another home."

Kerry stopped talking, unable to force any words past the large lump that lay in her throat. She looked down at the carpet where the shredded pieces of tissue lay around her feet like confetti.

2

As the ambulance men lifted the small body into their vehicle, which Crane now knew was a baby girl, he tore his eyes away from the poignant sight. His own son, Daniel was nearly a year old and he simply couldn't imagine life without his boy. By the look of him, Anderson, the father of two girls, felt the same, as he'd pushed his hands deep into his pockets and was looking away, down at the ground, as though the sight of the small body bag was too much to bear.

"What happens now, Derek?" he asked.

"What?" Anderson looked up. "Oh, there'll be a post mortem and an inquest. It depends on what the Major finds. If the baby died from natural causes then the case will be referred to the UK Missing Persons Bureau in Bramshill."

"Referred? What does that mean?"

"The details we have and a sample of her DNA will be logged on to their system and she'll be given a case number. They're the UK national and international point of contact for all missing person and unidentified body investigations. They provide support and advice to police forces in order to resolve cases and act as a hub for the exchange of information and expertise in this area. They also maintain the national database of missing and unidentified records. Then, after all the formalities are completed, Aldershot Police have an allocated corner of the cemetery where we bury unidentified bodies, so the baby will be laid to rest there."

Anderson took his hands out of his pocket to smooth down the grey wispy hair that matched his grey tweed jacket.

"Jesus," Crane said, shocked by the realisation that the baby could be buried, un-named and un-loved, in a bleak corner of the cemetery. He wasn't sure what he'd expected would be done but found the solution upsetting. He made a mental note to arrange a small ceremony for the child with the Padre at the time of the burial. He was determined the child should be laid to rest properly.

Forcing his mind back to the dilemma of identification, he said, "I guess they check their Missing Persons database?"

"Absolutely. But, remember, she may not be classified as officially missing. There are no babies reported stolen or missing at the moment in our area. If there were I'd already know about it."

"In that case," Crane said, "perhaps she died of natural causes and one of her parents left her here because they were too poor or too distraught to deal with the aftermath of death."

"Or, she was shaken to death or some such and was left here in order to avoid prosecution."

"Whatever the reason, it's all very depressing."

"You can say that again," said Anderson and he walked away towards his car, leaving Crane huddled in his dark suit. He watched the Padre and Kim walk into the church, their arms entwined, supporting each other and wished his wife Tina was there, offering him the same thing. But, that wasn't possible. And anyway he was a soldier. He was on duty. And he had to get on with the job. So he squared his shoulders and turned towards to his car, ready to drive back to Provost Barracks where he would write up his report on the morning's happenings and check on the progress of Billy's forensic examination.

3

Julie Wainwright hadn't had the best start to her day. As she rocked the baby in the gaily decorated bouncing chair with her foot, she mulled over the disastrous morning. The baby had been fractious and wouldn't feed properly, so by the time Bob had come down for his breakfast, nothing was ready. Since they'd been married last year, their habit had been to have a leisurely breakfast together on the days when Bob was off duty. Julie had tried hard to stick to this routine after Tyler had been born, but today it just hadn't worked out.

Sitting in a metal chair at their glass kitchen table, Julie had been unsuccessfully feeding the baby. She'd been dreading hearing Bob's footsteps on the stairs, as nothing she did to get the baby to suckle properly had worked. She'd taken Tyler off her breast, laid her over her shoulder and rubbed her back. Jiggling her nipple up and down in Tyler's mouth hadn't worked either. All Tyler had done, was to take a quick suck between screams, her blond hair going damp from the heat of her rage. Tears squeezed out of her tightly shut eyes and she waved her little fists in the air, as though wanting to pummel her mother for not being able to help her.

"What the hell's going on, Julie?" Bob had shouted over Tyler's screams, as he walked into the kitchen. "Can't you get the bloody baby to shut up?"

"Obviously not, Bob, or I would have done by now," Julie retorted, scraping back the metal chair as she stood up.

"Why are you down here with her anyway?" he'd asked. "You're supposed to nurse the baby in her bedroom. That's what I bought that bloody rocking chair for and you've hardly used it. Anyway, where's my breakfast?" he'd demanded, looking around the kitchen disbelief written all over his face because there wasn't one packet of cereal or piece of toast to be seen. Just pristine, empty, worktops.

Julie had decided it was best not to answer that question and turned and fled from the room, after mumbling, "I'll see if I can sort Tyler out upstairs."

It had taken 10 minutes of walking around, in and out of the three bedrooms and bathroom that comprised the upstairs of their Army quarter, all the while rubbing the baby's back, before the trapped wind had been released. During that time Julie had had to endure the crashing and banging from downstairs, as Bob was forced to make his own breakfast.

With the wind gone, Tyler had become drowsy, so she placed the baby in her cot, and watched amazed as Tyler had promptly fallen asleep, as though there had been absolutely nothing wrong with her for the past 45 minutes.

Julie had wished she could do that herself, as she'd collapsed into the rocking chair, taking a moment to compose herself. But such is the lot of a wife and mother and Julie well knew what was expected of her. So she prised herself off the rocker, braved the bathroom mirror and tried to do something with her appearance.

She rubbed damp hands over her dark hair, to try and tame the short tousled boyish cut, which had looked so much better in the hairdressers than it had ever done since. She rubbed some cream into her pale face and quickly cleaned her teeth before venturing back downstairs, with more than a little trepidation in her tread. Not that she was frightened of Bob. Well, not really. Only when he got like that. Annoyed. Distant. She just didn't know what to do for the best when he was in that sort of mood. Didn't know what to do to placate him. That was all it was. Just a bit of anxiety, she'd reassured herself.

Bob had looked up as she'd returned to the kitchen and then turned his attention back to his toast without speaking. She'd breathed a sigh of relief and thanked God that, for now at least, there was to be no more shouting. The silent treatment from Bob was much easier to live with than the shouting or criticism. Not that she believed in him – God. But he came in useful every now and then.

As she'd made her own toast, Bob's mobile had rung. He'd looked at the display, and then went out into the garden to take the call, where he'd paced around the small garden, his trainers getting wet from the damp grass. He'd come back indoors a few minutes later and begun gathering up his stuff. The keys to their car were stuffed into his jeans pocket, his wallet went into his back pocket, he'd strapped his watch onto his left wrist and grabbed his coat from the hooks next to the back door.

He'd still not spoken, so Julie, trying for a nonchalant tone said, "Where are you off to?"

She'd had to endure Bob looking her up and down, with what she thought was a grimace of distaste on his face, before he'd said, "None of your business." The blank look, which often meant 'whatever it is, I'm not going to talk about it', returning to his face after his scrutiny of her.

"How long will you be then?" Her irritation with him had made her brave and she'd pushed the point.

"As long as it takes," Bob had replied as he'd pulled on his coat and then slammed the front door behind him as he'd left the house.

After Julie had tidied up the kitchen, all the while refusing to give in to her sadness at the disaster area of her marriage, Tyler had woken up. So here she was, sat on the settee with a cup of coffee and Tyler in her bouncer at her feet.

She thought that maybe she'd get a chance to watch morning television and enter that day's competition where the prize was usually around £20,000. They could do with a few grand in the bank. Well who couldn't? Rocking the bouncer and reaching for the television remote, Julie had to admit to herself that this was nothing like she'd envisaged married life would be. Instead of being a devoted father, Bob seemed to have turned into someone she didn't know. His idea of fatherhood appeared to be to ignore the child as much as possible when he was at home, but boast about his beautiful daughter when he was in the Sergeant's Mess, surrounded by his cronies. So it fell to Julie to look after the baby on her own, irrespective of whether he was in the house, on duty, or during one of his long unexplained absences.

A knock on the door interrupted her reverie and her selection of the television channel. Her friend Linda opened the door and walked in. "You in, Julie?" she shouted and Julie heard the scrap of the baby carrier as Linda nudged the door open with it.

"In the living room," Julie replied brightly, but she was pissed off with Linda's belief that she could just walk into the house whenever she felt like it. Julie often fantasized about locking the front door to stop it happening, but she knew Linda would make so much noise trying to get Julie to answer the door by ringing the bell and hammering on the knocker, that Tyler would be rudely awoken from her morning nap. So she'd never tried it, not wanting to have to deal with the consequences of her actions. With a sigh, it occurred to her that she wasn't able to control her friends, as well as her husband.

"Morning, love," Linda said as she walked into the room, her brightly coloured clothes matching her bright mood. Julie had never seen anyone wearing purple leggings and a bright yellow shirt successfully before, but Linda managed to pull it off and had even topped the outfit with a yellow and purple printed scarf tied around her head, that held back her shoulder length dark hair. "I saw Bob leave, so thought I'd come round for coffee. Is everything alright?"

Knowing Linda was fishing for information, Julie simply said, "Yes, fine thanks, Linda. Bob just has a few things to do at work."

"I thought he was off duty today?" Linda asked as she lifted the baby carrier from her arm and placed her child on the floor next to Tyler.

"Well, you know how he is, devoted to his work and all that." Julie smiled warmly at her friend, trying hard to match Linda's sunny disposition. "Let me make you a coffee. Watch the babies will you?"

Julie made sure her smile was firmly in place as she stood. It only slipped when she walked into the kitchen and was out of Linda's sight. Julie was so tense, her whole body felt as stiff and unyielding as a block of concrete. Forcing her taut muscles to relax, she leaned against the kitchen sink. She didn't know what to do to make her relationship with Bob work, but the one thing she did know was she wasn't going to ask for help from any of her women friends on the garrison, no matter how nice they were. That was a sure way of feeding the ever hungry gossip machine and the quickest way to end her marriage.

4

Crane listened to the two men exchange greetings. They started moving along the path, both trying to look nonchalant, like it was common place for them to be walking in one of the local parks. Which, of course, it wasn't. The soldier had covered his regulation hair cut with a woolly hat and seemed to be trying to disguise his military bearing, by stooping down to the other man's level. The other man being a short, white, bulldog of a male, who Crane thought could be of eastern European descent or from somewhere in that area. Crane never could make head nor tail of all the countries that had broken away from Russia and become independent. And to be honest he didn't particularly care. He was far more focused on what was happening on his patch, with his soldiers.

Just then, their conversation was lost in a crackle of static, as a sudden gust of wind whipped up the discarded crisp packages, tissues and other pieces of light rubbish sending them whirling around the heels of the two men.

"Jesus, Billy, what the hell are you doing?" shouted Crane. He was sitting in the fake satellite company van.

Even though it was quite old, it acted as the perfect cover for covert operations in and around the suburban streets of Aldershot, for watching undetected and listening in to conversations. The supposedly mock dish on top of the van cleverly concealed a directional microphone and camera.

"Sorry, boss, it's very windy today. When a gust gets up sometimes it rocks..."

"Alright, shut up and get their voices back!"

As the static cleared Crane heard, "Got the sample?"

"Yes."

Bob Wainwright slid a packet, containing a sample of fine white powder, from the palm of his hand into the pocket of the other man's jacket.

"Good. I'll test it later. If it's as pure as you say it is, there won't be any problems. If it's not, then..." the recipient of the package let his words hang in the air.

"Then what?" asked Wainwright. A question that was rather superfluous in Crane's opinion, as he even he could hear the underlying threat in the voice of the Eastern European.

"Let's just say those who try and cross me don't live very long. Understand?"

The image on Crane's video monitor was so clear that he could see beads of sweat breaking out on Wainwright's forehead as he digested the threat. It served him right, Crane thought. He had no sympathy for soldiers who turned smugglers and was happy to see Wainwright squirming under the other man's hard stare.

"When is the shipment due?"

Wainwright stole a glance around the park, although there was no one else in the meagre space. The grass was sparse and brown due to lack of attention and the children's play area was full of broken and rusted equipment. The whole place was reminiscent of an area closed down for redevelopment. But Aldershot wasn't big on redevelopment, so it would probably be like that for a while yet.

"Soon," Wainwright replied.

"Soon isn't good enough. I need dates," demanded the contact.

"I'll let you know when I know, alright?" Wainwright drew himself upright.

If the soldier was trying to appear threatening it didn't work, Crane thought, watching the eastern European man laugh in Bob's face. "Dates, I want dates. Understand?" he said.

"I just told you, you'll know as soon as I know."

"Make sure I do."

Wainwright watched the man walk away with a look of distain on his face, more than likely at having to deal with the gangster, Crane thought. But Crane knew times were changing all over the country, not just in Aldershot. Heroin smuggling was as popular as ever, but now there were new gangs taking over the old territories. They brought with them fear and loathing. But that didn't seem to bother the eastern Europeans, they clearly weren't out to make friends, just lots of money.

"Do you want them followed, boss?" Billy asked as Crane pulled the headset off and put it down on the control panel.

"No, Billy. We know the deal is on and we've got a bloody good idea when the shipment is coming in, even if they don't."

Crane and his investigating partner, Sgt Billy Williams knew the drugs were coming thanks to the RMP on the ground in Lashkar Gah in Afghanistan.

They also knew the soldier based at Aldershot facilitating the deal was Bob Wainwright, but so far they hadn't been able to identify his customer. Now it looked as though things were finally coming together. So for the moment Crane decided it was a matter of waiting it out until the large consignment of vehicles repatriated from Afghanistan, as part of the British Army's successful withdrawal, arrived back in Aldershot. Hidden in that lot, somewhere, would be a large quantity of pure heroin. This was a golden opportunity not just for the villains (who were hoping to make lots of money) but for the Military Police, who wanted to break the drugs ring and Crane didn't intend to blow it.

"Come on, Billy, back to base. I need to get out of this bloody van."

Billy radioed to the spotters and told them stand down and then clambered though to the driver's seat. The creaky van sprang to life after a couple of false starts. As they drove back to Provost Barracks, the home of the Military Police on Aldershot Garrison, Crane watched the video clip again, then froze the screen and printed off the best shot they had of the unknown man's face, to show to DI Anderson. Crane was excited about this operation. A game of cat and mouse would make a nice change from the spate of murders and hierarchical bullshit he'd had to deal with recently.

When they arrived back at Provost Barracks, Crane got out at the car park and luxuriated in the cigarette he had been craving for the past couple of hours, before throwing the butt away and banging his way indoors.

5

Bob Wainwright settled in his chair in his sparse office on Aldershot Garrison and clicked the Skype icon on his computer. He pulled his chair forwards until he was sat at his desk, but as usual his knees banged up against the underside of the wood so he withdrew and turned his chair sideways to better accommodate his long legs. After a series of clicks and beeps the connection was made and the smiling face of John Davis filled the screen. Dressed in his desert combats, John looked far too happy for someone who had been on tour in Lashkar Gah for nearly six months. Perhaps it was the thought of all the money they were going to make that accounted for the grin on his face.

"How's things?" John asked, his voice sounding distant due to the dodgy connection usually prevalent when talking to Afghanistan.

Bob put on his headset needing to hear better. Not wanting to shout and be overheard he adjusted the microphone, pulling it close to his mouth. "Same old, same old," he replied.

"God you're a misery, Bob," John rebuked. "What's to be so upset about? If anything I should be the miserable one, stuck out here in the bloody desert."

"You don't have to deal with the people I have to," Bob grumbled. "And Aldershot is the fucking pits. Home of the British Army? That's a laugh. Home of the lost, broken and broke, more like. The High Street has more rubbish on the streets than goods in the shops."

"Never mind, you grumpy old sod, not long now."

"That's precisely why I'm ringing. What's the news?"

Sgt John Davis was in charge of the repatriation back to the UK of the last remaining personnel and equipment of his Regiment in Lashkar Gah and Sgt Bob Wainwright was responsible for accepting the returning men and goods into Aldershot Garrison.

The two had met when on duty in Afghanistan, which Bob had to admit was a rough old place indeed. The trouble with the desert was that it was too hot during the day and too cold at night. Plus, he'd never before realised how many places grains of sand could get stuck in, on and within the human body, causing much chaffing of the affected skin. But the main difference between there and Aldershot was that in Afghanistan at least you were doing a soldier's job.

He missed the adrenaline rush of his tour of duty over there and being back home had done nothing to fill the hole in his life that it had left in its wake. To be able to do the job you were trained for, was what Afghanistan was all about for Bob. But when he heard he was going back to the UK, with no chance of being posted back into a war zone, it had been time to make sure he was recompensed for the years of service to the British Army. The British Government were doing their best to make sure the lads didn't get the pension they were entitled to. Years of changing regulations meant that the pension that had lured him into the service in the first place had been diminished. Meaning his commitment to the Army and the regiment had lessened with every change. So he had quickly realised that it was up to him to provide a private pension of his own making.

He'd decided that if the stupid bastards were going to do him out of what he was due, he was determined to make up for it and had therefore jumped at the chance of making some extra money – actually a lot of extra money – when John had mentioned it one night, as they were bemoaning their lot.

The consignments of returning vehicles were their last chance to smuggle drugs out of Afghanistan and they intended to make the best of that chance. The plan was simple. The returning vehicles were packed with equipment, then weighed and stored securely whilst awaiting their turn on the large supply aircraft. Being the Sergeant in charge on the ground, meant it was a relatively easy thing for John to replace some of the returning ration packs on the vehicles with their own particular brand of sustenance. It was then a fairly simple matter for Bob to retrieve the packages once they were safely back in Aldershot.

Because they were unable to safely discuss which consignment the drugs were in, it was a waiting game for Bob. They had decided that as it was more than likely that every computer, mobile phone conversation, email and surface mail was monitored, no mention was ever made between them of the drug smuggling.

John had just confirmed the next load was due back in Aldershot the following week and Bob was really hoping there was something in it for him. So far there had been no ration packs anywhere. Plus he was getting bloody fed up with Josip Anic. The bloke was the most impatient man he'd ever met, making stupid threats if Bob didn't come up with a date for the delivery. He guessed it was because, for once, Anic wasn't in control. The trouble was, neither was Bob. They were both reliant on John Davis back in Afghanistan.

As Bob ended the call, having confirmed the vehicles were due for repatriation next week, he hoped to God this coming consignment would be the one with the drugs hidden in it.

6

"What do you think?" Crane asked Anderson, later that day, when he visited the detective at Aldershot Police Station and told him about the meeting he'd witnessed. "Do you recognise him?"

Crane handed Anderson the shot of the eastern European man who had met with Bob Wainwright, then removed his dark suit jacket and rolled up the sleeves of his white shirt. The heating in Aldershot Police Station had two settings, bloody hot or bloody cold and today was one of the hot days.

"Oh yes I certainly do recognise him," replied Anderson, after patting every pocket in his signature tweed jacket before finding and putting on his newly acquired specs and looking at the photo.

The spectacles made Crane smile, as Anderson still hadn't got the hang of his reading glasses. When he needed them he couldn't find them and when he had them on he kept forgetting to take them off before he got up and walked away, nearly falling over his feet in the process. It was shaping up for the specs to be another of Anderson's foibles, along with his badly stained tie and his penchant for sweet cakes.

"It's Josip Anic," Anderson continued. "A Croatian who came to live in Aldershot about five years ago. Since his arrival he's been building his businesses. He started with girls and then moved into drugs. His business plan is simple. He finds someone who already does what he wants to do, frightens the shit out of them and then takes them over. Works like a charm every time."

"Bit of a nasty bastard then," Crane took the picture from Anderson and studied the face. Anic certainly didn't look like anyone's friendly uncle. His features were so chiselled and hard it seemed as though he didn't know what a smile looked like, never mind had ever tried to pull his face into one.

"More than a bit," agreed Anderson. "He does the usual transportation of girls, putting them to work as prostitutes and we think he's responsible for most of the drug distribution chains from here to the coast."

"So most of Hampshire?"

"Yes. And that's a bloody large area, over 1,400 square miles. We think he smuggles the stuff in by boat, into a quiet cove somewhere along the long coastline. But, of course, we've never been able to get enough evidence against him for a prosecution. So he goes gaily on his way, making a bloody fortune and flooding Hampshire with harmful Class A drugs."

"Well, Derek, I think that's about to change, and for once it'll be us that gets the big payday," and he went on to tell Anderson about Anic's meeting with Bob Wainwright. As Crane concluded his retelling, Anderson decided the news called for a celebratory cup of tea and a couple of slices of cake.

Wedding

"The sun was shining on the happiest day of my life. The day you married me. Do you remember it?"

Kerry swung round on her computer chair to face Alan, a photo of the two of them in her hand. Preserved in a silver frame, she kept it on the desk next to her computer so she could see it as she surfed the net and tell him about interesting titbits she came across.

It was taken outside the Royal Garrison Church. He, resplendent in his Army uniform, all glinting buttons and rich colours and her in her white wedding dress, her ginger curls tied back with loose tendrils falling around her face and neck. The dress was artfully arranged around her and they were looking at each other full of love, hope and happiness. There hadn't been many guests, just Alan's family and some of his mates from the Regiment. Kerry's mum hadn't turned up. A blessing in disguise probably, Kerry realised, as she'd only have ruined everything by getting drunk at the reception and making a fool of herself. Kerry's mum couldn't resist a drink. Not ever.

"I'll tell you what I remember of it. It's like snatches

of a video that I can't seem to put together anymore. I'm just left with disjoined images. The standards hanging from the arched wall of the Garrison Church. The fragrance of the flowers that had been placed at the end of each pew. The Padre resplendent in his robes. The swell of organ music. And then us, spilling out of the church, into the bright sunshine. Holding hands. Stupid grins on our faces. Confetti softly floating down like coloured snowflakes, settling on us. Nestling in the folds of my dress. Landing along the shoulders of your uniform."

Kerry turned away from his chair and looked out of the window.

"The guard of honour was waiting for us. The lads from your unit so still, so stiff, so large somehow. They made me feel safe. Strong young men making an archway with their swords for us to go through. Defending us. Enclosing us. As we walked, the sunlight glinted off the ceiling of blades. Sending flashes of light in all directions, like lasers. Some reaching into the sky, some sending shattered sparks of light down upon us that mingled with the confetti. But as we left the safety of the glinting swords, I remember that the sun went behind a cloud and cast a black mark over us. As I turned and looked back at the lads from your unit, still proudly holding their swords aloft, half of them were also dulled by the shadow."

She went over to his chair and sat on the floor next to it. Leaning against one of its legs. Not wanting to lean against him. His battered and broken legs looked sore and she didn't want to hurt them. Yet she yearned to be close to him.

"Thinking back on it now," she continued, looking up at him, "the brave boys who were painted black by the loss of the sunlight, including you, were the ones killed by that bloody IED in Afghanistan."

She dropped her gaze to the floor and they sat in companionable silence. Contemplating how far the ripples of the disaster had reached, for it hadn't just ended Alan's life, but Kerry's as well.

7

Crane found the stark wording on the autopsy report didn't make the reading of it any easier. Not when the autopsy was on a three month old baby. Major Martin had been thorough in the extreme, but had found precious little. In fact the report had more negatives in it than positives.
Negative 1 – no failing of internal organs.
Negative 2 – no enlargement of internal organs.
Negative 3 – no toxic substances in the blood from a toxicology test.
Negative 4 – no broken bones, cuts, or bruises. In fact no trauma to the body of any kind.
Negative 5 – no identifying marks, blemishes or birth marks.
The only positive thing in the report was that the baby had been well nourished and clearly well looked after.

Forensic examination of the baby's clothes had produced one clear left hand index finger print on one of the tabs of the disposable nappy she was wearing which didn't belong to the baby.

The Major's conclusion was that the probable cause of the baby's demise was unexplained cot death. Which got Crane and Anderson absolutely nowhere. Billy had run a computer search, but there were no leads from the search of the finger print in their databases.

He threw the report back onto his desk in exasperation. He looked at his watch and saw it was time for him to meet with his new Officer Commanding, Captain Draper. Captain James Edwards, his boss for the previous 18 months had been transferred on and his new Officer Commanding, Dan Draper was the complete antithesis of Edwards. Where Edwards had been young, inexperienced, yet upwardly mobile, Draper was older, vastly experienced and had taken a commission after serving his 22 years, mostly in the Military Police, and achieving the rank of Warrant Officer Class 1.

On the one hand, it was a positive difference for Crane, as he found it much easier to relate to Draper and his experience in the Royal Military Police. Indeed he had great respect for the man's service record. However, he couldn't get over the hurdle of an NCO taking a commission. Normally the general consensus of opinion amongst Crane's peers about taking a commission was 'not on your bloody life'. But if Crane, later on in his career, wanted to stay serving in the Army until he was 55, he could feasibly attain the correct rank and then pass selection and be chosen for a commission.

Therefore Crane viewed Draper firstly with interest and secondly with a damn sight more respect than he'd ever had for Edwards. All the formal hand over from James to Draper and the 'meeting the team' bullshit had been done a few weeks ago and things were now starting to settle down into the normal routine, part of which was Crane keeping his boss up to date with ongoing cases.

After all the Army rigmarole had been dispensed with, Crane sat in front of Draper's desk in silence for a few moments, while his new boss read the autopsy report Crane had just handed him. The salt and pepper short haired head shook in dismay as he put the papers down.

"Well, that gives us absolutely nothing to go on, Crane," he said. "I understand we've not got any decent leads from the CCTV cameras either. Several women can be seen walking around with prams that morning but as there isn't a camera trained on the entrance to the church, we don't know which one, if any of them, went inside. And anyway we've only shots of their backs and grainy black and white photos at that."

"I know, sir, that's why I want to look elsewhere."

"Where is elsewhere?"

Crane would normally have received a look of distain from Edwards at this point in their meeting and was glad to find an enquiring, interested look from Draper instead. His naturally arched eyebrows rising above crinkled eyes and square chin.

"I was thinking of exploring the Army connection."

"By that I take it you mean the fact the baby was left at the Garrison Church?" asked Draper.

"Exactly, sir. It's the only thing we have to work on really."

"And just how do you think you might identify any soldiers whose wife may have had a baby three or four months ago?"

"By checking those lads who have taken compassionate leave or paternity leave, whatever you want to call it." Crane received a small frown from Draper and immediately said, "I obviously include female soldiers who have taken maternity leave, in the general term of lads, sir."

Crane was glad of his short beard at that moment as he hoped it had helped to mask his embarrassment as his face flamed.

"It means running a few searches to see what we can find," he continued after a brief pause, "and perhaps narrow things down, but we should be able to come up with a list of those who have recently become fathers or mothers on Aldershot Garrison. I'd also like to include surrounding camps, say Arborfield, Borden, Deepcut, Bisley and Odiham."

A slow smile started on Draper's face and brightened his brown eyes. "Nice one, Crane. Let me know if anything comes from it. Dismissed."

"Thank you, sir," replied Crane, standing to leave.

"Oh, by the way," called Draper.

"Sir?" Crane stopped by the open office door.

"For goodness sake, call me boss, or Draper will you, Crane? You can even call me Dan when we're in my office. Or anything you like, as long as it's not a swear word. Okay?"

"Okay, boss," said Crane and his smile matched Draper's as he left the office, impatient to get Billy searching their computer system for likely suspects.

Abandoned

Kerry lay on the settee, staring up at the ceiling. "Empty - that's my life now, Alan," she said. "Bloody empty. I've got there now. The bottom of the pit. And let me tell you it's not very nice down here. It's bland and boring. Grey and fuzzy. There are no colours here. No sunlight. No laughter. No emotion. Life's just a flat line with no ups or downs in it."

Her words echoed through the silent, sparsely furnished room.

"I'm finding getting into a new routine difficult, you know? A new routine without Molly in it. So I'm carrying on with the old one. Getting up in the morning at the same time I used to when Molly needed feeding. But instead of my darling nuzzling at my breast, there is nothing. No one. Just emptiness. I am as empty and devoid of emotion as I am of milk, so I just sit and stare out of the window and watch everyone else getting on with their lives."

She swung her legs off the settee and stood up. She hadn't bothered to get dressed yet that morning, so was still dressed in one of Alan's tee-shirts that she had worn to bed. She liked to wear them, imagining they still had some of his scent caught in the fabric, although they had all been washed and ironed many times since he'd last worn them.

Walking over to the window in bare feet she stumbled under the weight of her grief. Catching hold of the sill to steady herself, she said, "Look at them. The people down there on the streets. They're like ants, scurrying here, there and everywhere. They all seem to have something to do. A reason to get up in the morning. It doesn't matter if they like or hate what they do, they still have to get out of bed and get on with it. So I get up as though Molly was still here. As though I had a reason for living too."

She looked over at Alan, immobile in his chair, his Army uniform as tattered as her life. Crossing the room she climbed onto his lap, curling into a ball like a cat, embracing the smell of smoke, heat, sweat and death emanating from him.

"I've never heard from my mum, you know," she whispered, as if telling him a secret. "I rang her when you died. Left a message about when the funeral was. But she never showed up. Never even rang me back. That's my mum. Not that she was much of a mother. Mother in name only really. Let's face it she's married to the bottle. Always has been. Always will be, I expect. No wonder my father left her before I was born.

"I used to fanaticise about who my father was," she confessed. "Saw him as this kind, caring, individual who was looking for me. Trying to find his little girl. Trying to get back to me. But looking at the wreck of my mother, I can't imagine anyone liking her enough to have any sort of relationship with her. Maybe she was a lady of the night and that's how I came about. Maybe the story of my father leaving her and me was just that.

A story."

She stirred on Alan's knee, wriggling around to get more comfortable. Wishing he would put his arms around her, comfort her, but they stayed immobile by his side.

"So when I met you," she carried on, "I couldn't understand what you saw in me. No one had ever seen anything good in me before. Obviously my mother didn't. I was just in the way to her. At school I was largely ignored, as I couldn't keep up with the other kids who had parents at home who cared. Who helped them read. Explained tricky maths problems. Watched them practicing for drama class. I was always the one left out of sports teams. The one forgotten about. The one child never picked by the teacher to do something nice, or responsible. But you didn't leave me out of your life, did you? You invited me in and then let me stay. You were interested in what I had to say and how I looked. I had finally left my old life behind.

"But I should have known it wouldn't last. Because you abandoned me as well, didn't you? Okay so it wasn't your conscious decision. You didn't deliberately drive over that bloody IED. You really did want to come back home. Back to Molly and me. So I guess it's not your fault. But it's so hard to deal with, Alan. So hard to cope with. My mum and dad left me. You've left me and now our baby's left me. She must have preferred to be with you rather than me."

She raised her head and looked up at him, his shocked reaction to the explosion still frozen on his face. "How do I get over all that?" she asked him. But he didn't reply.

8

As Crane looked around the room with a possessive air, his uppermost thought was that he loved his job. He'd faced some troubles during his stint at Aldershot and more recently, in the process, ending up on the wrong side of those of a much higher rank than himself. But in the end it was Crane who had prevailed and was still at Provost Barracks, reaping the benefits of his struggles.

The team were discussing the drug smuggling case they were investigating, that he'd dubbed 'Operation Repatriate'. A corny name, he knew, but what the hell. Other suggestions had been as equally idiotic, so he made the unilateral decision to go with his own suggestion.

He listened to Billy outlining the current 'eyes' on Bob Wainwright. A round the clock rotation of Branch and RMP soldiers was in place and working well. Crane had been concerned that Billy may have been affected by the loss of Kim from the team. Even though they hadn't been particularly close as individuals, they had worked well together from a professional point of view and Billy seemed to be feeling that loss. Kim had always been the one constant in their investigations. No one else had come close to her devotion to her duties and the strong, quiet calm she had brought to the office. Not forgetting her investigative insight, which often came from her methodical cataloguing of garnered information. As a result of that loss, Billy seemed slightly wrong footed. Crane hoped that by giving him extra responsibility in the drugs investigation, he would rise to the challenge.

Billy was followed by DI Anderson who talked the team through the Aldershot police surveillance on Josip Anic. The background to the man was fairly standard. A Croatian, who was a small fish in a big pond in his own country, had come over to England to try his luck. God knows why the man had chosen Aldershot. Crane couldn't see the attraction himself, but over the past few years Anic had extended his reach throughout the whole of Hampshire. As was usual in these cases, no direct evidence had ever been found to charge Anic with. Not for drug offenses, nor for inflicting grievous bodily harm on, or even killing, his rivals, although the Police knew all three illegal activities had taken place. Anderson had managed to charge a few of his foot soldiers and had successfully taken them off the streets, but there were always more to take their place and so the illegal business went on, gaining momentum, like a giant snowball rolling around the county, flattening everything in its wake.

As Anderson wrapped up his presentation and put his reading glasses away in the breast pocket of his jacket, Crane got ready to give his briefing on the timescale and details for the next consignment of returning vehicles. Crane looked around the room and saw the empty chair on which Kim would have been sitting. They were awaiting the appointment of a new

Office Manager, meaning Billy and some of the others had to carry the extra work load. But the nubile Sue from the RMP office next door was still doing her best to help out at particularly busy times, much to Billy's delight. Crane didn't think Billy wanted a relationship with her, he just enjoyed the view.

Standing and walking to the front of the room, he looked at the assembled men watching him. Billy was blond haired and muscular, wearing his dark suit and white shirt as befitting a Branch investigator. Bald headed RMP Staff Sgt Jones was in his preferred uniform of fatigues. Finally there was the grey haired, greyly dressed Anderson, a senior CID officer with the Aldershot Police. They had all worked well together in the past, despite, the interference by their Officer Commanding, Captain Edwards. Now, Crane believed, they were set to be a complete and formidable team, with the recent appointment of Captain Dan Draper. Crane was determined to show his new boss how efficient and effective they could be. He wanted them to stand out from other Branch teams and this was their big chance. Crane would do his utmost to ensure they brought the investigation in on time and on budget, as the saying went.

"Right." Crane paused to make sure he'd got everyone's attention. "The next consignment of vehicles from Lashkar Gah is due in next week. It's a clutch of land rovers which will be packed full of stores and other equipment that needs returning to the UK. The RMP in Afghanistan reckon this will be the last big chance for smuggling the drugs out of our part of Afghanistan. We anticipate heroin in large quantities. We have men working undercover with Sgt John Davis in Lashkar Gah and others keeping an eye on the vehicles identified as part of the next shipment. We expect the drugs to be concealed in ration-pack boxes. At least that's the word from Afghanistan. Apparently Davis has quite a few empty boxes stored in a locked cupboard in his office. Once of the lads caught sight of them, when he surprised Davis by walking into his office unannounced. Hopefully we'll get photos of Davis stashing them in the Land Rovers. We've already got photographic and voice recording evidence of him meeting the suppliers and are anticipating being able to document the hand over from the Afghanis to Davis.

"Boss?"

"Yes, Billy?"

"Once the consignment leaves Lashkar Gah, will the RMP be arresting Davis?"

"No. Not until we're ready to go at this end. We don't want to give Wainwright any reason to panic and decide not to retrieve the drugs. We need all that photographed and documented, as well as his handover to Anic. This is one of the biggest drug sting operations the RMP have done in a long time and we're determined to get every link in the chain. And I mean every link. So no loose talk, chatting in the Sgt's Mess, telling the wife, alright?"

"Boss," Billy and Jones agreed.

"The arrests both in the UK and in Afghanistan will be co-ordinated, all taking place at the same time as we arrest Wainwright and Anic at the hand over. Through our surveillance of Wainwright, we'll know the time and place of the meeting. Anything else you want to add, Derek?" Crane asked.

"Not really, just to say that the undercover lads in the Drugs Squad are also monitoring Anic and his cronies, as well. We've decided the more police that know what's going on the merrier. Can't do any harm and hopefully may help."

"Just so long as Anic and his men don't realise they are being watched."

"Well, to be fair they expect surveillance to a certain extent, which is why I got the Drugs Squad involved. They need to know what's going on so they don't inadvertently balls up Operation Repatriate. Also if Anic thinks it's business as usual with the Drugs Squad keeping an eye on him, he's not going to think that anything out of the ordinary is going on. We don't need Anic spooked."

As they dispersed, Crane walked out with Derek to the car park, where he lit up a cigarette before sauntering over to the DI's car with him.

"Well, it seems that everything's in place, Crane," Derek said.

"Yep. Just a matter of waiting it out now," Crane smiled.

"Are you alright, Crane?" Anderson asked peering at Crane's face.

"I'm fine, Derek, why?"

"Because you're too bloody cheerful," Anderson laughed and turned to unlock his car. "It must be the X-Edwards factor."

"Ha bloody ha," said Crane but with a wide grin on his face.

"Seriously though," Anderson said through the open car window, after he'd climbed in, "It's nice to work with you in an upbeat mood for once."

"Instead of?"

"Instead of your usual dogged, dour and distracted demeanour," and Anderson grinned at the rude finger sign Crane flipped him, as he drove away.

9

The sermon he was writing was uppermost in Padre Symmonds' mind and he belligerently answered the phone call that had just broken his concentration. He had to move some papers he was referencing to find the offending instrument and was annoyed that he'd lost his place.

"Symmonds," he barked, but realising how he must have sounded he quickly added, "How can I help you?"

"Good morning, am I speaking to Padre Symmonds of the Aldershot Garrison Church?" a young woman's voice asked him.

"Yes you are. To whom am I speaking?" he asked rather formally, on his guard until he knew who he was speaking to and what it was they wanted.

"This is Diane Chambers, Padre."

"I'm sorry, but I don't believe we know each other."

Francis knew exactly who she was, but had no intention of telling her that. He leaned back in his comfortable leather office chair, sinking into the squidgy leather and bouncing lightly on the rocking mechanism. The chair had been his indulgence, when he put together his home office. As he spent so much time sat behind his large desk, dealing with all his paperwork, he'd decided he needed a good chair to sit in.

"I'm from the Aldershot News, Padre and I wondered if I could ask you about the dead baby you found on your church steps."

Francis winced at the 'dead' bit. The woman could have been a bit more tactful, he thought.

"I believe you should be speaking to the Aldershot Police or even the Royal Military Police, not me."

He picked up his pen and started to turn it over and over in his hand.

"I already have talked to them, sir," Diane said. "I just wanted a personal perspective from you. For my readers, you understand. So I can write a rounded piece."

Padre Symmonds well understood that the last thing Chambers ever wrote was a rounded piece of journalism. But now she had him on her hook, so to speak, he'd have to respond somehow. But not knowing the best way to deal with her, he kept quiet for the moment, waiting for her to speak again.

"I understand you and your wife found the child," she said.

"Yes, that's correct."

"It must have been a shock."

"Obviously. It would have been a shock for anyone, Miss Chambers." Now he sounded as though he were addressing a child and he knew he had to try for a more normal tone of voice.

"Your wife, Mrs Symmonds, nee Weston, was in the RMP serving on Aldershot Garrison, wasn't she?"

"I really don't think that has anything to do with anything, Miss Chambers." Francis struggled to be polite to the obnoxious woman.

"It's just that I was wondering if I could have a quick word with her."

"I'm sorry, but she's not here at the moment," he lied, crossing his fingers to try and negate the slip in his moral code. "Why on earth would you want to talk to her anyway?"

"I just wondered if she'd consent to being interviewed. I'm doing an article on working women and it would add to the piece if I could talk to a woman who used to serve in the Army and ask how she feels now she's become a wife and retired early, as it were."

"I think you'll find my wife will decline to be interviewed." Francis sat upright and laid the pen he was holding down on his desk.

"Surely, that's a decision she alone should make don't you think? So would you be kind enough to pass on my message?"

"Very well," Francis tried to swallow his anger, without much success.

"My telephone number is…" and Chambers went on to recite her office and mobile numbers, neither of which Francis took down. The pen remained on his desk, where he had just put it. "Thank you," she concluded.

"If there's nothing else, I'll bid you goodbye." He really had had enough of her and her stupid questions and ideas.

"Just one last thing, sir, could I have a quote from you?"

"A quote?" he repeated stupidly.

"Yes, about the matter of the child being left on the church steps."

"Oh, very well," and the Padre rattled off a quick

sentence for the woman to put in her article about how poignant the leaving of a dead child, on the steps of the church, was.

"Thank you very much for your time, sir and your quote. Especially as the police and the RMP declined to be interviewed," said Chambers and cut the line before he could react.

"Bugger! Talk about being wrapped up like a kipper," he said into the now dead phone and replaced the receiver.

"Kipper?" Kim asked as she walked into his study. "What's that all about? Surely you're not talking about kippers in your sermon this Sunday," she laughed.

"No. It was that bloody awful woman from the Aldershot News on the phone. She just got the better of me and I ended up giving her a quote about the baby found on the church steps last week."

"Did you say anything out of turn?"

He thought for a moment, "No I didn't think so, let's just hope she writes what I actually said."

"Never mind, Francis, you're not the first of her victims and I doubt you'll be the last."

"Talking of victims," he said, "she's got you in her sights," and he gave her the message Chambers wanted him to pass on, minus the phone numbers. "What do you think?" he asked when he'd finished.

"About giving her an interview? Not on your life."

"I know that, Kim, but what are your thoughts on the question she posed?"

But Kim merely smiled and said, "Can I get you more coffee?" and she collected his mug, turned away from him and returned to the kitchen.

"Bugger," he said, for the second time in five minutes, as he watched his wife leave the room.

10

The chatter washed over Julie as she sat in the Mother and Baby Group, with Tyler fast asleep in the baby carrier by her feet. Tyler had fallen asleep in the car and Julie had managed to get her out and carry her into the local community centre without waking her. She settled in her usual place on a comfy settee near the coffee bar and looked around. The other mothers scattered about the echoing room, were busy feeding their babies, playing with them and one or two were changing them. Not having any of those things to do Julie smiled down at Tyler and let her thoughts wander. And they wandered to Bob, as they usually did these days. She wriggled in her seat and pulled her skirt down, studying the black ballet type shoes she was wearing over black tights. Her shoes were losing their sheen and the patent leather was beginning to crack and split where they bent as she walked. They were beginning to look unloved. Just like she felt. Definitely unloved. She couldn't quite identify when things had begun to go wrong with their marriage, but somehow the downhill slide seemed inextricably linked to her pregnancy.

Bob was already in the Army when they'd met and

as the relationship became more serious, he'd told her he was a career soldier. There was no negotiation about this, no chance that he'd change his mind. He was in it for the long haul and if their relationship was to progress and last, she'd have to accept that and become part of Army life. From what Julie had experienced of the life by that time, she was happy to comply. She loved the companionship and camaraderie between the men, which also extended to their wives and girlfriends. There was always something to do; someone to meet, a dinner to go to, or friends calling round. And drinking. Lots of it. Some of it hard core. But the wives and girlfriends were mostly left out of that. A pastime reserved exclusively for the men, for when they needed a blow out. They all seemed part of one big happy social club.

Bob was great while she was pregnant. He was attentive, proud and looked out for her and after her. Well, she supposed, thinking back, he did get a bit fed up with the fact she couldn't drink alcohol, but she tried very hard not look bored, or tired, on those nights when the drunken antics went on into the wee hours of the morning. Tried hard not to let it show on her face. Even if that was how she felt inside. Sometimes she succeeded. Sometimes she didn't. She soon learned to succeed, though, after enduring his alcohol induced wrath. Not that he ever touched her. Never hit her. But then he didn't need to. His tone of voice and words were frightening enough. Enough to control her.

Things had got better again after the baby was born. For then she could join in with the social life, the drinking and the banter. Sometimes they had people around, or went round to friends, all the babies safe asleep up stairs. Occasionally babysitters were organised, as a night on the town was in order. So life had gained some sort of equilibrium once again. Some of the wives had asked her recently if her and Bob were going to have another child. A lovely brother or sister for Tyler. The thought of it made Julie shudder.

"Hey, girlfriend," Linda elbowed her in the side as she settled next to Julie on the sofa, placing her baby carrier on the floor in front of her. "Are you okay? You seemed miles away then."

"Sorry, just thinking."

"About your Bob?"

"Mmm," Julie kept her voice light.

"Bit of a hunk your Bob," Linda's eyes sparkled. "Lucky you, that's what I think."

"I know exactly what you think of him," Julie smiled without rancour, "I've seen you flirt with him often enough."

Linda laughed. "It doesn't mean anything, you know. We're just having a laugh. I'd never do anything about it. You do know that. Don't you?"

"Yeah, course, I'm just winding you up," and the two women shared a complicit smile.

Just then Tyler started grizzling, so Julie scooped her up and put her over her shoulder, rubbing her back for comfort. It seemed to work as Tyler's eyes fluttered closed and her head lolled against Julie's shoulder as she fell back asleep.

"What would we do without them, eh?" Linda said.

"Without who? Our husbands or our children?"

"Well, both, but I was thinking of the babies."

"Why, what's brought that on?"

"Haven't you seen the local paper?"

"No," replied Julie, "not yet."

And Linda went on to tell her about the child found

dead on the Garrison church steps last week. Julie held her baby just that little bit tighter. She thought she'd feel as if her heart had been ripped out if she lost Tyler. Bob might seem a bit distant with the baby at times, but she was sure he'd feel the same. Wouldn't he?

Aldershot News

"Morning, Alan," Kerry called, as she came into the flat and hung up her coat. "Look, I picked up the local newspaper today, while I was out shopping. I thought I'd read it while I have a cup of coffee. I can read some interesting bits out to you, if you like. Do you remember how we used to do that? Read to me, you'd say. Because you loved listening to my voice, you'd say. Personally I think it was to help me with my reading. A nice way of encouraging me to better myself. And it was working too, wasn't it? So I'll keep up with the practice. Buy the local paper every week and read it out loud to you, if you like."

Going into the kitchen she put the kettle on for her coffee. "Mind you," she called through to him, "I try not to go out too often, as I don't want to get stopped by someone wanting to see the baby. If they do, I think I'll say she has a bad cold and I don't want her exposed to any more germs. Or, I've just got her to sleep, so I don't want her disturbed, as she's had a bad night. Or, I haven't time to stop as we have a doctor's appointment. Yes. Anyone of those reasons should do it."

Kerry took a used mug which she had left near the

kettle last night, rinsed it and spooned coffee in it, ignoring the pile of washing up that had been festering in the sink for the past few days. She sniffed the milk she'd just taken out of the fridge and decided it was fresh enough to use, splashing some into the mug before pouring hot water onto the brown swirling concoction.

Standing and stirring her drink she said, "Mind you, what if more than one person stops me? I'll have to remember which excuse I used. Then again, I don't know that many people. But a lot of people chat to you when you've a baby, you know. It's a bit like when you have a dog. Other dog owners talk to you. Ask questions about it, or tell you all about their dog. It's the same with a baby. If you are pushing a pram or pushchair around, other women stop to chat, pass the time of day, compare notes, that sort of thing."

She carried the coffee back to the sitting room and sat next to the newspaper she had thrown on the settee, placing her mug on the floor.

"I expect it's because it can be quite lonely at times, being a mother at home. Especially if you're used to company at work and then all of a sudden you're pushed into being alone in the house with a screaming baby for most of the day. And most of the night, come to think of it, if the father's away, like you were, or doesn't give a shit and would rather be down the pub. So, yes, other mothers are often desperate for someone to talk to who understands."

Whilst she flicked through the newspaper she carried on talking to Alan. "I never found it lonely, though, being a mother," she said. "It was as if I was meant to be one all along. I was so excited about being given the chance to treat a child properly, after being treated so badly myself. No way would I ever have put Molly through the experiences I had. But I didn't get much time with her, did I? I only had a few short months to show her how much I loved her. To show her that she was the most important person in my life. Oh, sorry," Kerry's hand flew to her mouth. "I should have said that you... and... her... are the most important people... in my... life."

She couldn't stop her voice breaking and she stumbled over the words. She took a gulp of coffee in an effort to compose herself, before she gave up trying and broke down in tears.

"Yes," she sniffed. "I know I should have said 'were' the most important people in my life, not 'are' but I need to believe you are both still with me."

After a pause she continued, "Sorry, I shouldn't have gone there. Memories like that make me upset. Bring it home to me yet again that the two most precious gifts I had are gone. Gone, together, to some place without me. To a place where I can't follow. At least not yet.

"I've often thought about ending it, you know," she looked across at Alan, who was sitting in his chair looking as stiff and uncomfortable as if he were a visitor, rather than her husband. "Ending this loneliness. But what scares me is that if I take my own life, I'll be sent to someplace else. Not to the place where you two are waiting for me. Because it would be a sin, see. Suicide. You didn't sin as you gave your life for your country. Molly didn't sin as she was an innocent child who just wasn't meant to be on this earth for very long.

"So," she said, forcing a brittle brightness into her voice, "I mustn't end it all. No matter how much I want to. I have to try and be strong for both of you. Try and get through the days, months and even years until we can all be together, as we should be. A family. Anyway, that's enough of that. Let's see what's in the paper."

She set her mug on the floor and put the newspaper on her lap, turning it back to the front page.

"Oh my, here's a report about Molly. About how she was found and who found her. They're appealing for information. What? Oh, sorry, Alan, I'll start at the beginning and read it to you.

BABY FOUND DEAD AT LOCAL CHURCH

A baby girl was found abandoned on the steps of the Aldershot Garrison Church last week by the Padre, Captain Symmonds. The baby was pronounced dead at the scene.

Police have not yet been able to trace the parents, although enquiries are ongoing. In the meantime they have issued an appeal asking local residents to be vigilant and let them know if a family who had a baby, now doesn't. "It's a very sad situation," Detective Inspector Anderson commented. "The death of a baby is always tragic and we are, obviously, trying to trace the parents. At this moment in time we feel it could be that the mother, or father, are ill or destitute. We won't know the exact cause of death, until the results of the post mortem are known, but initial findings indicate the baby died from natural causes."

Padre Symmonds was also said to be "extremely concerned" for the parents of the baby and urged them to get professional help, to support them through this terrible time.

The baby was described as around three months old with fair downy hair, blue eyes and a bow shaped mouth. She appeared to be well nourished and was dressed in clean clothes. No distinctive marks were found on the baby who could have died 12 to 24 hours previously, meaning death occurred sometime during Monday night.

If anyone has any information that may help the police, they can call them, in confidence on...

Kerry fell silent. The harsh reality contained in the article hung between them. After a while she found the courage to speak again.

"Wow. That was a hard read. Not because the words were difficult, but because the words were difficult, if you understand what I mean. I could read them easily enough, I just found it hard to find my voice. Sorry, I faltered quite a lot through that, didn't I? I wonder why..?" she fell silent again.

"Sorry. I was lost somewhere then. What did you ask? Oh, you wanted to know what I going to say? Well, it sounds stupid now, but my initial thought was - I wonder why they didn't put her picture in the paper, then everyone could have seen how beautiful she was - then I realised that they couldn't. Couldn't put a picture of a dead baby on the front cover of the Aldershot News. That never would do. So they printed a picture of the Garrison Church instead. Without Molly by the door, of course."

11

The local paper slid off her knee and fell to the floor, as Kim Symmonds let go of it and leaned back against the settee. She'd been reading the article about the baby they'd found at the Garrison Church. She was trying to work out how she felt about not being part of the investigation. Not working with Sgt Major Crane, DI Anderson and even the Major anymore. She also missed Billy. Missed his stupid humour and his attempts to draw her into the social life of the Branch. But on the other hand, she also knew she'd have missed Francis more, if she'd decided to stay in the Military Police and ended her relationship with him. Not married him. At the end of the day that just hadn't been an option and the thought of his love made her smile.

But she knew Francis worried about how she felt now. He wanted - no, scrub that - needed reassurance that she was happy and felt she had made the right decision. Well, she couldn't worry about his insecurities. After all she'd married him, hadn't she? That should be reassurance enough, she reasoned. For now she needed to focus on herself. Focus on her role as the Padre's wife. Focus on what she felt she could actually give - as opposed to what was expected of her.

Over the past few months since they'd been married, she'd 'got over the God bit' as she'd put it, at the beginning of their relationship and now had no trouble in accepting that she shared his faith. Not to the same degree, perhaps. But enough to accept her husband's calling.

The problem for Kim just now, was that there were no 'duties' for a Padre's wife. It appeared that everyone did whatever best suited their gifts, personality and situation. She knew there were some wives with jobs outside the home. In fact, she'd been talking to one who had just completed her nursing training. So Kim had to figure out what activities best suited her own gifts. What role she could take on that would make a difference. She knew she couldn't just bumble along being the Padre's wife, answering the phone, taking messages for him and keeping his diary up to date. She'd had a well-defined role in the Army and couldn't shake that need. So it was up to her to find her own calling. Find her own well-defined role in civilian life.

She picked up the remote control and switched the television on. For now, she was watching re-runs of the hilarious television sitcom, 'Rev'. An irreverent look at being a vicar in an inner London parish. But of more relevance to Kim, was the fact that he was married to a woman with her own job. So, as she watched the programmes, Kim focused on how his wife coped with being married to a vicar. Providing support to her husband, whilst not being involved with his work. Kim knew that to most people learning how to be a Padre's wife from a television programme was bizarre in the extreme, so she kept her guilty secret to herself.

But along the way she was also learning what it was

like to be a vicar today. Learning that it's not all just seriousness, sermons and prayers. Learning that there is comedy in life, juxtaposed with the pathos of the calling. Understanding that Francis was a decent person trying to do good. Doing the best he could to support his lads and their families. Whether he was here in Aldershot, out on exercise, or on tour in war zones.

Most importantly, Kim was fast learning that being 'the Padre's wife' was a huge privilege and that the blessings far outweighed the challenges that accompanied the role. So she put her legs up on the settee, picked up her cup of coffee and settled down to enjoy the first episode of the second series of Rev.

12

"I'm getting sick of these bloody meetings you keep calling for no apparent reason," Bob Wainwright hissed at Josip Anic, as he stooped down to the other man's ear. Then he straightened up, regaining his military bearing and continued, "I've nothing to tell you. The stuff will be here next week but I don't have the exact date yet." He stuffed his hands in his coat pockets and stared down at Anic.

"I just need to keep reminding you of your obligations, that's all," the Croat smiled and with his small dark staring eyes, set behind bulbous cheeks, he reminded Bob of a hypnotic coiled snake, ready to pounce.

"I know my bloody obligations," Bob said. "I just think you're taking unnecessary risks with all these meetings."

He looked around the motor vehicle body shop in exasperation. He was standing with Anic in a small glass walled office which gave a sweeping view of the industrial unit and the open garage doors at the front. There were what appeared to be two spray booths at the rear of the large space. Their walls reached to the ceiling and both had a large industrial sized silver tube snaking out of the side wall, funnelling up through the ceiling to the outside. Wainwright presumed these were to clear the air of paint droplets from the spraying process. The opening of each spray booth weren't doors, but thick strips of cloudy plastic that reminded him of extra large fly screens. The air inside the office and the rest of the industrial unit was heavy with the smell of paint thinners and was so thick Bob was breathing in short shallow gasps and would have welcomed a paper filter mask to wear.

"What risks?" said Anic. "You've simply come to the body shop for a quotation to repair your damaged body work."

"What damaged body work? I don't have any damage on my car."

Anic looked through the large window and nodded to a thick set man who was standing next to Wainwright's car. Bob followed Anic's gaze just in time to see the man kick a dent in the offside wing.

"That damage," Anic said conversationally. "Now if you'll just wait a few minutes, my man out there will give you an estimate for the repairs."

"You little shit, you…" The icy stare from Anic stopped Bob adding more expletives, so he settled for, "Leave my car alone and leave me alone," said as threateningly as he could manage, as a small sliver of fear poked through his anger, making him realise he'd better rein in his temper.

"And what if I don't?" Anic shrugged. "What are you going to do?" and he smiled his reptilian smile. "The only way to keep me appeased is to keep me abreast of developments. And if that means meeting me when I tell you to, then that's what you'll do. Or should

I let a local police snitch know that you're able to obtain cut price Army surplus gear. You've got a nice business going on in the sidelines, I hear. A business that I think you really wouldn't want the police, or the military police, to know about. And that's not to mention the drug smuggling."

Wainwright silently fumed. Bloody Croat. Worthless piece of shit, he thought, but he was sensible enough to keep his mouth shut and his thoughts to himself.

"Now fuck off," Anic said, dismissing him as though Bob was nothing more than a turd on his shoe. "I'll let you know when we'll be meeting again."

Wainwright looked through the glass windows at Anic's four men. They were all holding a tool of some sort and they were all staring at him. Bob flung open the office door and deliberately slammed it behind him. The man who had kicked Bob's car, walked to meet him and held out a piece of paper.

"Your estimate, sir," he said in his thick Eastern European accent.

Wainwright snatched the piece of paper from him and stormed out to his car, chased by brays of laughter from Anic and his men. Once in the driver's seat Bob unfolded the paper. Scribbled beneath the body shop logo were the words, "I own you."

Screwing up the offensive piece of paper and tossing it onto the back seat Bob started the engine, stamped on the accelerator and with his wheels spinning, fish-tailed out of the yard.

eBay

Kerry had come to a decision. Not one made lightly, but born of necessity. She was finding it very upsetting to see Molly's things all around the flat. They were a constant reminder of her loss and of her failure as a mother.

"I've decided to sell some of Molly's stuff," she told Alan. "I've got to be careful as I still want people to think I have a baby. But I can sell some of her clothes and toys. Best keep the pram and possibly the highchair. I need that around just in case anyone calls. And if they want to see Molly I can just say she's sleeping in her cot and I don't want her disturbed."

Kerry moved over to the computer and switched it on. "What did you say?" she asked him. After listening for a moment, she retorted, "Look I know I don't have any visitors, don't rub it in. But one day I might. Who knows if social services will call round or someone from the local council. I wouldn't put it past that nosey old cow of a social worker to turn up any time she liked."

Kerry had still not forgiven the woman for the way she treated her after Alan had died. Okay she'd found her this flat, Kerry had to give her that. But she treated her with distain. To her Kerry just seemed to be another piece of paper. She was surprised the woman hadn't rubber stamped Kerry's arms as well as the handful of blessed forms authorising this, that and the other. Shaking away the recollection, her ginger curls bouncing like coiled springs, she carried on.

"Anyone in authority can call whenever they feel like it, so I have to be prepared, Alan, so yes, I'll definitely keep the high chair. And I always take the pram with me when I go out."

She carried on chatting to him, glancing at his chair every now and then from where she was sitting at the computer, which was placed on a small table in the corner of the room.

"I can't risk someone seeing me on my own and asking awkward questions about where Molly is. I've taken to wrapping one of her blankets around a towel so it looks like there's something in the pram that could be a sleeping baby."

She looked closely at the computer screen for a moment, making a couple of failed attempts before she got the password correct for her eBay account.

"Right, I've logged onto eBay, let's see what I can find. Mmm...baby clothes is the category I want. I better click on that and see what people are selling similar stuff for, then I can price mine right. It'll also tell me how much postage people charge. I don't want to get that wrong. If it's too much people won't buy the items and if it's too low I'll end up using the money I get for the stuff to pay for the postage."

Kerry fell silent and for a while all that could be heard was the clicking of the keys on the keyboard. The empty room seemed to amplify the noise, making the clicks and clacks sound like a grandfather clock, patiently ticking out the passage of time.

"Oh for God's sake, bloody internet," Kerry broke the silence. "I seem to have gone onto the wrong category. I've got baby dolls, not baby clothes. I better try again. Oh, hang on, wait a minute. Come and look, Alan. These dolls look so real. There's quite a few on this seller's site. All different ones. Oh my goodness they look alive! And they have movable arms and legs. Let me just scroll down and have a look at some more...look, they've all got their own names. Violet, Blossom, Snowdrop. Oh for goodness sake, Alan, what's the matter with you? I asked you to come here and you're still sat there. I suppose I'll have to bring the laptop to you."

Kerry scooted over on her computer chair, laptop balanced on her knee and stopped next to Alan's seat.

"Sweet Jesus, that one's called Molly, Alan! It looks just like her doesn't it? Look there's her little button nose. And her lips aren't white anymore. They're a lovely shade of pink. See, there's a bloom to her skin, she's not grey anymore. Her lovely downy blond hair is styled just right and her arms and legs can move. She's not stiff and dead anymore."

As he hadn't bothered to look at the laptop screen, she lifted it off her knee and thrust it in his face.

"Look Alan! It is Molly I tell you. Stop it! Stop saying it isn't. Stop saying it's just a doll! I'm not going to listen to you no matter how loud you shout."

Kerry put the laptop back on her knee.

"I wish I could touch her. But the screen's in the way. Molly, oh Molly, mummy misses you so much. Is this how you'll manage to come back to me? Oh dear, I've put huge hand prints all over the screen. I was just trying to touch her. Get close to her. I'll use this tissue, it's wet with my tears so that should clean it. There, that's better. I can see her properly again now."

Kerry got up and put the laptop back on the computer table, her hands shaking a little from the emotional release after the shock of having found Molly.

As she went back for her chair she said, "I don't care what you say, Alan, I'm buying her. I must before someone else does. I'm not going to bid, I'm going to press the 'Buy Now' button and you can't stop me. Get away, leave me alone. Molly needs me!"

She rolled the chair back to the table, sat down and clicked on the large pay button on the eBay page.

"There I've done it! I said you couldn't stop me. Now shut up while I arrange payment and delivery. I better not sell her stuff now. She's going to need all those baby clothes to wear and her toys to play with. Oh Alan, you don't know how happy it's made me feel. Molly's coming back to me and now life will have some purpose again, some meaning. What do you think, Alan?"

She turned and looked at his chair, expecting to see him still sitting there, but he'd disappeared.

Reborning

When Kerry woke the next morning and staggered half asleep towards the kitchen to make a cup of tea, Alan was back. She breathed in the familiar smell of smoke that rose from his singed uniform and smiled. She'd known he wouldn't leave her on her own for long.

Once she was settled on the settee with her drink, she grabbed some pieces of paper that she'd printed out the night before.

"Listen to this, Alan. I looked up reborning on the internet. I thought I'd research it while we wait for Molly to arrive. I didn't have anything else to do as you'd buggered off and left me on my own. Anyway, enough of that, I don't want us to quarrel today, I'm too happy. So, did you know reborning dolls first started in America in the early 90s? That's what it says here. Listen, I'll read you a bit: *Existing dolls are repainted and then the artists add human hair and eyelashes. The dolls are weighted to resemble new born babies and their heads need supporting giving the feel of a real baby.*

"No wonder they're expensive," she said, "What with all that painting and adding real hair! My goodness, I wonder how the artist knew to make the doll look like

Molly. Perhaps Molly came to her in a dream, or something. That way she would have known what Molly looked like. Then all she had to do was to advertise the doll so I'd see it. Yes, Alan, that must be it. What?" she listened for a moment. "Well can you come up with a better explanation?" she said. When he didn't answer she continued, "No, I thought not, so shut up and let me read the last bit to you. Just listen to this: *All dolls were originally made from regular baby dolls, hence the term reborning - making an existing doll come to life.*

"See, I was right, Alan, it is Molly, she has come back to life. She's been reborn and she's found her way back to me. I can't wait to hold her in my arms again. To sing to her, rock her to sleep, dress her in her pretty clothes."

Kerry mimed rocking Molly in her arms. Something that was as natural to her as breathing.

"Why am I crying? It's alright they're tears of happiness, Alan. My prayers have been answered. Molly has been reborn and is coming back to life." Kerry continued rocking. "I knew I was right to place Molly on the church steps that day. Ever since then I've prayed and prayed that God would hear me and bring my little girl back."

With a sigh of satisfaction, Kerry let go of her dream, stopped rocking her baby and retrieved her mug of tea from the floor.

"Anyway, you can leave me alone for now. I've got to get on with sorting out Molly's things and make sure the bedroom is clean and tidy for when she comes home. I've got some of her clothes that need washing. I hadn't been able to face doing them before, but I must now, Molly's going to need them. So off you go, back to where ever it is you come from. But don't forget to come back later," she called to him as he began to shimmer and then faded away, leaving behind a few wisps of grey smoke.

13

Crane, eyes pushed tightly against a pair of binoculars, watched from the roof of a nearby barracks, as Bob Wainwright, ant-like below, logged in the latest vehicles to be repatriated from Afghanistan. The sun was being chased across the sky by clouds and Crane was glad that at the moment they'd caught up with it, throwing the roof into shadow and lowering the temperature.

The line of Land Rovers snaked up to the weigh station, where Wainwright stood with his clipboard, recording the receiving weight of each vehicle. Crane was watching for any changes in Wainwright's composure, which might indicate which vehicles contained the contraband. But so far, nothing. Wainwright was either a bloody good actor, or he hadn't found the tampered vehicles yet.

The sun had beaten the clouds away and was streaming down onto Crane's back, his black suit absorbing the rays and raising his temperature further. He would love to crawl back from the roof's edge and take his jacket off, but didn't want to miss anything, despite the fact that Billy was next to Crane, recording the proceedings with his digital video recorder. And then it happened. A stiffening in Wainwright's body as he looked at the manifest on his clip board. The manifest for each land rover contained a detailed account of the contents packed within it. Crane imagined he saw a slight smile flit across Wainwright's face, before the man bent his head once more to his task.

As Crane watched, the waiting soldiers, at Wainwright's command, moved to the vehicle. One was accompanied by a beautiful German Shepherd, trained in finding explosives, which sniffed its way around the outside of the land rover. Others checked under it with mirrors attached to poles and the last man popped the hood and checked the vehicle's VIN number (the vehicle's unique identifying number) against his own list. Once they were satisfied, the driver was given permission to move the vehicle away, parking it in the secure compound a few hundred yards away and then the whole procedure started again.

Satisfied, Crane succumbed to the heat and slipped away from the edge to take his jacket off and grab a few well deserved gulps of water.

"How's the resolution?" he asked Billy as he sat up in between swigs of water. "Is the video going to be clear enough?"

"Spot on, boss," Billy replied without taking his eyes from the camera. "The test shots I did before the land rovers started arriving showed nice sharp pictures, even from this distance."

"So there's going to be no disputing the evidence that it was Wainwright checking and clearing the vehicles?"

"None whatsoever, boss. You can count on it."

"Good. Carry on, Billy, I'll be back later."

Crane moved across to the small brick structure which marked the entrance to the roof from the floors below. Waiting for him there were Draper and Anderson.

"All good, boss," Crane said to Draper and got a satisfied nod in return.

"What happens now?" asked Anderson.

"A rotation of spotters will move across to the other side of this roof to monitor any activity in the secure compound over night. They'll stay in place in case Wainwright comes to collect the drugs. If he collects them, we'll follow him to see where he stashes them."

"When do you think he'll come, Crane?" Draper wanted to know.

"Difficult to say, boss. Maybe tonight, but on the other hand he could wait a while. The land rovers are expected to stay put for a few days, as the lads take their cooling down period and adjust to the transition from Afghanistan, before they're expected to get back into their normal routine here in Aldershot."

"Very well, keep me posted," Draper said. Turning to Anderson he asked, "Is there anything else you need to see, Detective Inspector?"

"No thank you, sir, you've been very helpful."

"Good. I want to foster a good relationship between the Army and the police. Personally I feel that for too long there's been a misconception by the military that everything they do should be kept secret from the local police. I don't hold that view and, as you know, neither does Crane here, so if we can do anything else to help - within reason, of course," Draper said, "just shout, okay?"

"Okay and thanks again."

Draper and Anderson shook hands before the new

boss of the Branch left them to it.

"Bloody hell, he is a bit different from Edwards isn't he?"

"I told you he was," smiled Crane. "But..."

"But?"

"Well at the moment he's walking the walk and talking the talk, let's just hope that doesn't change."

"As distrustful as ever, Crane. Don't you ever change?"

"Not that quickly," smiled Crane. "Anyway, I've got to arrange the spotter teams, so let's get back down to earth, shall we?" and the two men walked into the stairwell and clattered their way downstairs.

14

The realisation that their smuggling plan was now a reality, had just hit Bob Wainwright and he staggered into his office on unsteady legs and fell into his chair.

Imagines of huddled conversations when he'd finalised the plans with John Davis, all those months ago, flashed through his mind, as though he were watching a television drama or a film. He saw Davis' infectious grin and recalled the back slapping as he'd said, "It'll all go like clockwork, just you see. What could possibly go wrong?"

Even though their plan seemed to be intact so far, lots of stuff could still go wrong, Bob knew. Now it was time for him to keep his nerve and not be side tracked or riled by anyone or anything. If ever there was a time for military precision, this was it. Not forgetting military stoicism. Davis had managed everything his end without detection, so Bob couldn't let him down and balls it up here in Aldershot.

He was just beginning to calm down when his mobile rang. He didn't recognise the number, but that didn't mean anything. He suspected it was Anic calling for an update, from one of the many disposable mobile phones he used once and then threw away. Wainwright thought this was all a bit melodramatic, even gangster like, but then again Anic definitely fancied himself as a gangster.

Pressing a couple of keys on his phone, he said, "Yes?"

"Hi Bob, 'Good As New Body Shop' here. We have an available slot for your car repairs, this week. When would you like to bring it over? We could do later today or tomorrow."

Dear God, thought Wainwright, what was the man on? Perhaps he'd been taking a bit too much of the cocaine he so enjoyed peddling.

"So, when is best for you?" Anic pressed. "Today or tomorrow?"

"I'm a bit busy at the moment," Wainwright said, playing along and trying not to laugh. "Might be a few days yet. I've got a lot on at work. Why don't I give you a call when I'm ready to come over and see if you've a free slot then?"

"Are you sure? We really would prefer today or tomorrow." Anic's voice had hardened. No more the fulsome garage proprietor.

"Absolutely, sure, I'm afraid. Not to worry, I'll be in touch," and Wainwright closed his phone, shutting Anic up and shutting him out of his thoughts. For the moment Bob's efforts had to be focused on remaining normal at work. No one must see him preoccupied, looking worried or anxious. Looking down at his uniform shirt, he decided a trip to the locker room was in order. He needed a clean shirt, one that wasn't stained with sweat.

The minute Bob pulled up in front of the house that

evening, he realised he'd made a mistake coming home instead of going for a drink in the Mess. The baby was not just crying, but screaming, great big lung-full's that could be clearly heard from outside. He considered getting back in the car and driving away, but at that moment Julie came to the window and saw him. Damn, he realised he'd been caught and slammed the car door closed before striding to the door. As soon as he reached the step, the door was flung open, revealing Julie standing there her clothes and hair in disarray with the screaming baby perched on her hip.

"Thank God," she said, "here," and pushed Tyler towards him. He had no option but to grab the screaming child, who didn't moderate the volume of her screams at all with the change of parent. He held her close, before realising the child smelled. A lot. Of vomit and something too disgusting to even think about.

"Julie, what the hell?" he said, holding Tyler away from him.

"Look, just bring her upstairs for me," she shouted over the din. "If you hold her just for a minute while I get the stuff out and get myself organised, it would really help. Well, are you coming?"

He stomped up the stairs behind his wife, annoyance in every step.

"How did you manage to get in such a state?"

"Who are you talking to?" Julie said as she went into the nursery. "Me or Tyler?"

"Both of you. You women are beyond me. Why couldn't I have had a son? Boys are much easier."

"And how would you know?" Julie pulled open drawers and collected clean clothes for the baby.

"Well, that's what they say."

"Who?" She ripped open a new packet of nappies. "Your cronies down the Mess?"

"Yes, a few of them have babies now."

"Whose wives look after the babies, not them."

"Well, we do have to work you know," he laid the baby down on the changing mat at Julie's nod.

"Oh yes, provide for the little woman at home. Fulfil your role as macho men."

"What's got into you, for God's sake," he shouted, just as the baby shut up, making his voice come over more strident and demanding than he'd intended.

Not surprisingly Julie bit. "What's got into me? What's got into you, more like. You're never bloody here and when you are, you don't pay us any attention."

"What the hell am I doing now, then?" he shouted back.

"Helping under sufferance. Anyone would think you had another woman the way you're carrying on."

Tyler was now quiet and snuffling, so Julie popped a dummy in her mouth and laid her down in the cot.

"Another woman?" Bob said. "What on earth are you talking about now? Don't be so bloody stupid," and he went to leave the room, then thought better of it and whirled around. "Is that all you have to think about? Wondering if I'm having an affair? Don't you know me at all?"

"Well what is the matter then?"

"Work, just work, Julie. The only problem is pressure of work. I'm very busy at the moment."

She shoved past him out of the room and padded down the stairs, going into the kitchen. As he followed her, she grabbed the kettle and started to fill it with water.

"What pressure of work is that, Bob?" she asked

over the noise of the water hitting the inside of the stainless steel kettle. "I thought it was just a matter of logistics, bringing back all the stuff from Afghanistan."

"Just a matter of logistics? You stupid cow. You haven't got the first idea have you? Just a case of logistics, my arse. Have you any idea how many men and how much equipment we're repatriating? No," he answered his own question. "You've no idea. All that's in your head is stupid thoughts about me having an affair. For God's sake, pull yourself together woman."

"Pull myself together?" she shouted as she grabbed two mugs out of the cupboard and began savagely putting coffee in them. "I think maybe you should be taking a bit of your own advice, Bob. Now look who's over reacting."

"Jesus," Bob shook his head. "I just don't need this right now, Julie. I don't want any bloody coffee. I'm off upstairs for a shower and then I'd like some dinner when I come down. So wind your neck in and get on with what you should be doing. Being a wife and mother."

He walked out of the kitchen slamming the door behind him, which was just as well as he heard a coffee mug smash against the closed door, instead of into the back of his head. He ran up the stairs and when he reached the bedroom he slumped down on the bed and looked at his hands. They were shaking. He knew he had to keep it together and hoped a shower would help to calm down him down. If only Julie would keep her bloody mouth shut, he'd be able to get through the next few days. And then everything would be alright and they'd be set for life.

Funeral

Kerry was busy cleaning the flat. She had to make sure everything was ready for Molly's arrival. She'd changed the sheets on the cot and then after looking at the state of the grubby pillows and torn duvet on her own bed, ferreted out some clean linen she'd put away in the wardrobe and never used. As she shook out the sheet and then the duvet cover, puffs of dust rose in the air, disturbed from the surfaces of her bedside table and dressing table. The furniture didn't match. Not much in the flat did.

She picked up an old rag she was using as a duster, flicking it this way and that across her bedside table and sprayed polish on the dirty marks from mugs put down without coasters, rubbing away at them without much success. She moved to the dressing table and caught sight of herself in the large mirror. She turned one way and then the other, looking at her profile, trying to decide which was her best side. She realised she didn't have one, for both looked as bad as each other. Her figure was now model thin. But she decided she was no Kate Moss as she was more skeletal thin, than svelte. She seemed all bones. Thin arms poked out of her short sleeved jumper and even the size small leggings she was wearing looked baggy. She knew it was about time she starting looking after herself, especially now Molly was coming back.

The thought of a re-born Molly cheered her and she looked down at the items on the top of the dresser, ready to dust those. She'd made a little shrine for Alan, with candles either side of his regimental photo and the flag his coffin was draped in. She picked up the flag, careful not to unfold it and as the material slithered under her fingers, her happy disposition slid away, as she fell into her memories of Alan's funeral.

The baby had cried as hard as she had, that morning. But Kerry had been incapable of comforting the child - needing comforting herself. So in the end they both cried all the way through the brief service at the graveside, for the only person who could have comforted them was no longer able to. She remembered standing, swaying over the open grave. She was sure she would have fallen in, if someone hadn't grabbed her from behind and led her away.

She'd kept turning her head, back towards the grave, where men were now starting to fill in the hole. She could hear the thud, thud, thud of earth as it fell onto the coffin, making her think that Alan was alive in there, banging on the lid, wanting to get out. She squirmed out of the embrace of Alan's friend and made to run back to the grave to help him. But strong arms enfolded her once more and led her gently but decisively onwards towards the car. She tried to protest, to tell someone that Alan was trapped in that awful box, being buried alive. But everyone just shook their heads at her and told her it wasn't true. She'd never really believed them. Until now. Until she'd seen with her own eyes the state of his poor broken body and knew that he couldn't have survived those injuries.

Kerry stayed sitting on the bed, holding the flag until it grew dark and the temperature in the flat dropped, the cold causing goose bumps on her arms. She reverently replaced the flag on the dresser, pulled on her thick dressing gown over her clothes and left the bedroom to go and make a hot drink.

15

It was well after midnight. Bob Wainwright lay in bed, checking and rechecking every small detail in his mind. He'd been meticulous in his planning for the retrieval of the drugs and thought he'd covered everything. His palms were itching and his ears burning. Was there someone out there talking about him? Were his palms itching because of all the lovely money he'd have very soon? Unable to lie still anymore, he slipped out of bed. Julie had fallen asleep beside him about an hour ago, so he reckoned it should be safe to leave the house now. He just hoped the bloody baby stayed asleep. If she woke up, Julie would soon see he wasn't there and want to know what the hell was going on when he got back indoors. Or worse still come and find him. And he didn't need the added complication of a reaction from her. He was damn sure it wouldn't be a supportive one, especially as she'd got it into her head he was having an affair, as she'd told him a few days before. He still hadn't been able to appease her on that point.

He made it downstairs, with the clothes he'd worn that evening, a black pair of joggers and polo shirt to match, tucked under his arm. He went into the kitchen and quickly changed. Going out of the front door and closing it ever so slowly behind him he ran to his car, which he had parked on the drive as normal. He took the packages out of the boot, stacking them on the driveway, wincing at the noise of the boot closing.

He raised the garage door as quickly as he could with the minimum of noise. But still the clanking of metal and screeching of pulleys echoed around the street like rumbles of thunder. It was just his luck that he didn't have a door in the back of the garage that would have been easier and quieter to open. Not wanting to put the garage light on and alert his neighbours to his presence, he took a small torch out of his trouser pocket.

John's idea had certainly worked so far, he had to admit. Every nook and cranny aboard the jeeps being repatriated had been packed full of stores and then driven onto the Hercules cargo plane. Part of the payload aboard the vehicles was a contingent of ration packs, which were used for those soldiers who were on operations away from base and not able to return for food. Individual ration packs were put into larger boxes, each holding 12 ration packs. This full box weighed 12 kilos and 6 ration boxes had been packed into each land rover. Davis had simply taken the ration packs from these larger boxes and replaced the contents with 12 kilos of drugs. Therefore one of the Land Rovers contained 6 tampered boxes of ration packs. 72 kilos of heroin that was destined for Josip Anic, to be poured into his distribution chain throughout the South East of England, with a street value of millions of pounds sterling.

Bob Wainwright's job was simple. Being in charge of unloading and packing away the stores, he had just said (and noted on the manifest) that the bloody idiots over there in Afghanistan had packed 6 large boxes of rations which were out of date. Wainwright therefore had no choice but to destroy them as they were no longer fit for human consumption. But instead of destroying them, Bob had kept them locked in a cupboard at work and moved them to his car a couple of boxes at a time and from there into his garage. This was the last of them. All he had to do was to stash these two boxes safely in his garage, undetected.

Crane had been messaged a few minutes ago by Billy telling him that Wainwright appeared to be moving the drugs. He'd taken to sleeping in his clothes for the last couple of nights as he wanted to be there when Wainwright was seen moving the last of the shipment from work to his home. The night was cloudy, as though there were a lid on the sky and Crane hoped it would help muffle the noise of his arrival. He crouched down as he approached the car in which Billy was watching Bob Wainwright's house. After he settled himself in the passenger seat, Crane looked through the eye piece of the camera set up on the car dashboard, careful not to touch it with his hands and dislodge the stand.

"I followed him with the camera as soon as he came outside, boss," Billy whispered. "Damn shame we can't arrest him now while he's putting the packages in his garage. Get the thieving, dealing, bastard, red handed."

"Now, now, Billy. You know we can't. We have to get Anic as well, on the hand over. Anderson deserves that."

"As long as nothing goes wrong, boss. What if this turns out have been our only chance of catching him and we've let him go? How are we going to feel then?"

"It's not going to happen, Billy. Stop worrying. We have to trust the police on this one. They'll make sure there are no mistakes. Anderson's trusted us enough in the past, now it's time for us to pay back that trust."

Crane understood Billy's frustration, indeed felt a bit of it himself. But agreements were agreements and he wasn't about to double cross Anderson.

By now Wainwright had finished putting his packages in the garage. They hadn't been able to see anything inside the garage itself, just the wavering of his torch as he moved around the space. Once all the boxes were in the garage, Wainwright appeared outside again and cautiously closed the large up and over door before slipping back into his house. As there was nothing more to see, Crane left Billy mumbling away to himself about wasted opportunities and all the things that could go wrong with the plan to arrest everyone involved at precisely the same time.

Crane wondered if the stupid bastard, Wainwright, realised he was getting away with this just a bit too easily. Wondered if he had any notion that he was being allowed, by the military police, to retrieve his drugs and sell them on, so they could build a water tight case against him. The thought of the co-ordinated arrests to come made Crane smile as he reached the end of the street and hurried around the corner to where he had parked his car.

Delivery

Kerry was dozing on the settee when her mobile rang. Her eyes blinked in time with the merry tune that had disturbed her, as she fought to clear her head of the miasma that had been enveloping her for the past few days. Alan hadn't been around whilst she'd been getting ready for Molly's arrival and that had been the problem. She'd missed him terribly, his absence stirring up those awful yet familiar feelings. She was bereft, unloved and lonely. Kerry considered not answering the phone as she couldn't imagine who would possibly want to call her. She had no siblings, nor any real friends. She had acquaintances, she supposed, other mothers from the mother and baby group for instance, but none of them had her number. And she hadn't seen any of them since Molly died. Well she couldn't go there with an empty pram, could she?

That was it - Molly - Kerry realised, as the fog in her brain slowly cleared. It must be about Molly! Kerry grabbed at the phone, but merely succeeded in knocking it off the low table. Rolling off the settee and dropping onto the floor, she found it next to one of the legs and frantically opened it, desperate to answer the call before it stopped ringing and went to voicemail.

"Hello," she said, her hand trembling in anticipation of the news she hoped the caller would be bringing.

"Mrs Chandler?" a male voice called. "Express Deliveries here. You're expecting a package?"

"Yes, yes, that's me. Where are you? Are you here? Are you downstairs?"

The male voice laughed. "You seem keen," he said. "Yes, love, I'm here at the entrance to the flats. Can you come down? You see I've got a bad leg and…"

"Yes, yes, stay there, I'm coming, don't leave, wait for me," Kerry said as she grabbed her keys off the kitchen worktop and opened the door.

"Right oh, love, thanks," he replied and ended the call.

Oh my God, oh my God, Kerry thought, as she flew along the landing. She ignored the lift, preferring to brave the stairs. It would be quicker than waiting for that old cranky thing, she decided. She ran down the six floors without incident, her slippered feet slapping against the steps, the shirt she was wearing over a tee-shirt billowing behind her. No one was there to see her frantic flight as not many people tended to be around mid-morning. Those who could get out, generally went out and those who couldn't were engrossed in morning television. There wasn't much on the TV in the afternoons though, so that's when the housebound took up their posts at their windows. Or opened their flat doors, pulling up a chair and sitting in the doorway, in the hope of seeing something or someone worth watching, just to break up the monotony of their day.

The cheerful driver called to her as she pushed through the entrance door and beckoned her over to his van, holding out a large rectangular package. She grabbed at it greedily, scribbling something on his electronic pad that looked nothing like her signature and then held the package protectively to her chest. She nodded her thanks to the driver as she wasn't sure she could manage a civil conversation and breathing hard, carried her package back to the entrance to the flats. Not wanting to do any damage to Molly, she decided to use the lift on the way back up and as she waited, after pushing the button to call the lift, she tapped her foot in frustration at the slowness of the contraption.

While she was waiting she looked more closely at the box. It was wrapped in brown paper, with her name and address written on a piece of notepaper torn off a pad and stuck down with tape. There were also several 'fragile' stickers in red on it and the plastic covered delivery label of the courier service. Once inside the lift, Kerry held the box to her ear, to see if she could hear Molly inside and then chastised herself for being so stupid. Molly would be fast asleep, she reasoned, needing to be woken by her mother, like Sleeping Beauty waiting for her Prince.

The obnoxious journey up six floors was over at last and she breathed in the cleaner air as she stepped outside. Not that the air was much better up on her floor, as there was a light mist curling around the blocks of flats that morning. She opened the door with her key and stepped carefully through, not wanting to jolt Molly and give her a fright. As she looked up, she saw Alan waiting for her in his chair.

"I knew you'd come back," she said excitement bubbling in her voice. "Knew you wouldn't miss Molly's arrival. Now just wait there, while I carefully unwrap her."

Kerry placed the box on the low coffee table

between them and went into the kitchen, rooting around in several drawers before she found a pair of scissors. She eyed the mess of unwashed crockery, some of it covered in half eaten food and vowed to clean it up later, when Molly was asleep in her cot. Now the baby was back, she couldn't risk her coming into contact with germs.

She cut the paper off the box with unsteady hands, worried that she might inadvertently pierce the box and harm Molly. Once the paper was off, she lifted the lid on the cardboard box. Inside were mounds of polystyrene chips, which she scooped out and piled on the floor around her, slowly revealing the sweetest sight she had ever seen. There was Molly, eyes closed, dressed in the most gorgeous pair of pink pyjamas, nestled in a blanket. With trembling hands, she scooped her up, putting one hand under her body and the other under her head. As she placed Molly in the crook of her arm and supported the weight of the baby and her head, she immediately felt her tense body relax. All the horror and worry of the past few weeks seemed to fly out of her as the maternal yearning for her child was sated.

She was captivated by the reality of the baby girl, who was truly a marvel. Kerry brushed her finger across the baby's exquisite face and then caressed her delicate wisps of hair. She touched Molly's hand and moved the tiny supple fingers and finally ended her examination at her tiny wrinkled feet. Molly was, at last, back, snuggled happily in her mother's arms and holding her protectively, Kerry walked over to Alan.

"Look, Alan," she whispered, "Molly's home."

As she held Molly up, the baby's eyes opened and looked directly at her father. Kerry swore she saw his eyes glint and widen in pleasure at the sight of his child, before the light faded from them and they turned opaque once again.

16

Julie dragged herself off the settee in the lounge and went through the house towards the kitchen. She had to make a start on dinner, otherwise Bob would be home and there'd be nothing for him to eat. She wasn't in the best of moods tonight. Tyler had been fractious all day. The baby was over the colic that had blighted the first few months of her life, but now she was grumbling and crying for no apparent reason. Julie wondered if she might be teething, as her bottom gum was a bit red. If it's not one thing, it's another, she thought.

As she walked past the mirror in the hall she stopped to look at her reflection, then wished she hadn't. Her short dark hair was doing it own thing as usual and was just an unholy mess, her skin had lost its glow (if it had ever had any) and she had deep craters under her eyes. All signs of tiredness. But Julie didn't need to look in the mirror to know how tired she was. She felt it in every movement of her body. A body that had all the speed of a sloth. And when she tried to read or watch the television, her eyes would close of their own accord and she would then be jolted awake by dropping her book, or starting at a loud noise on the television programme she had fallen asleep in front of.

Pawing at the kitchen wall, she found the light switch and flicked it. But instead of the light coming on in the room, she was startled by a large bang as the bulb failed. What else could go wrong today, she wondered and as her eyes filled with tears she slumped against the wall, giving in to her emotions for a moment. Then taking a deep breath she blinked away the stupid tears and tried to drag up some positivity from within. She'd just have to get a new bulb and put it in, she decided. She knew Bob had some in the garage.

The garage was Bob's domain and Julie didn't often go in there. It was his bolt hole and he had spent many hours putting up shelves, organising his tools and creating storage space for all those things they needed to keep but rarely used. He'd told her that the spare bulbs were in the grey metal cabinet against the back wall, so as she heaved at the up and over garage door, she knew exactly where she was going and strode confidently through the organised space. She grabbed at the handle of the cabinet and turned it. But the handle wouldn't move. Not if she turned it to the left. Nor if she turned it to the right. Bloody hell, she thought. There are times when she wished Bob wasn't so organised, careful and pedantic. She couldn't imagine why he would lock a cabinet that just contained spare bulbs, batteries and boxes of screws she grumbled to herself as she went back indoors to grab her keys. At least he was organised enough to have given her a key for the cabinet.

Rushing back to the garage, for by now she was running very late and wanted to get the vegetables peeled before Tyler woke up or Bob got back, she picked through the keys until she found the small silver one that opened the cabinet. Slotting it into the lock she turned the key and then the handle, with a small sigh of relief, as it moved easily in her hand.

The bulbs were located on the top shelf and she found one easily enough. As she was about to close the door, she noticed the remaining shelves were not packed with the usual batteries, screws and nails, but with what looked like Army supply boxes. Frowning in confusion and reading the print on the boxes, she couldn't imagine what on earth Bob wanted with what appeared to be out of date Army rations. Pulling a box off the shelf, she wondered if there was anything in them that was of any use, for surely not all the contents would be out of date.

Julie was surprised to find how heavy the boxes were and put her bulb back on the shelf so she could grab the nearest package with both hands and placed it on the floor. Kneeling beside it, she ripped off the tape sealing the two flaps closed. Inside were separate ration boxes and Julie picked up the nearest one. Once again ripping the tape off the top, she opened it, intrigued as to what was in the meal packages. But instead of the packets of dried food she was expecting, there was just a solid block wrapped in what appeared to be some sort of aluminium foil. Perhaps this was a new type of food? Maybe it contained strips of pepperoni or other such disgusting dried meats. She knew soldiers would eat anything whilst on exercise or on patrol. Picking at the piece of tape sealing the side, she managed to grasp the flaps of foil. As she prised them apart, instead of strips of food falling out, fine white powder peppered the floor.

She licked her finger and went to put it in the powder. Not sure why she was doing it, but she'd seen people do it in the movies, when testing the quality of illegal drugs. And that was what she strongly suspected this was.

As she stretched her wet finger towards the stuff on the floor, she was startled by Bob shouting, "What the fucking hell are you doing?"

Shopping

Kerry had spent the last couple of days enjoying her family time with Molly and Alan. She had concentrated on getting Molly into a routine. An early morning feed, change of nappy and clothes, followed by a short cuddle with her father, before going down for her morning nap. The afternoons were livelier. That's when Molly would lie in her play pen between her parents, surrounded by her stuffed animals and rattles. Alan normally watched her then, so Kerry could do some housework. She was careful to keep the flat spotlessly clean now that the baby was back and Alan was encouraging her to do the chores by helping out with looking after the baby.

Kerry wasn't sure that Molly was up to a bath in the evenings, so she cleaned her with baby wipes, changed her nappy and put her in her sleep suit. Kerry brushed out her beautiful hair, gave her the last feed of the day and then it was time for bed, after a night-night kiss from Alan. Kerry was as happy as a princess in a castle, with a handsome prince by her side.

But today she had to leave her fairytale world, as she needed some shopping and after getting herself ready by changing into a clean jumper and leggings, she poured Molly into her outdoor jump suit and put her in the pram. Kerry changed her slippers for a pair of boots and then they were ready for the off. Kerry invited Alan to go with them, but as usual he preferred to stay at home. Stay sitting in his chair, where he would wait for them to come back.

Kerry chatted away to Molly on the short walk to the shops, enjoying the wind in her hair and sun on her skin even though it was chilly. She pointed out places they'd been before and described some lovely baby clothes she saw in a shop window, but couldn't afford to buy. She wasn't sure Molly was listening, though, as the motion of the pram seemed to have sent her to sleep again. Her lovely eyes were closed and the sight of her long dark lashes made Kerry proud that her baby was so beautiful. Molly still had that lovely bloom to her skin and her fine curly hair was just peeping through the hood of her jump suit.

The local supermarket was small by comparison to the big Asda in Farnborough and Tesco in Aldershot, but it stocked a wide enough range of basic supplies and the prices weren't too bad. As she wandered through the aisles picking up staples such as tea, coffee and milk, other shoppers looked at the pram and then smiled up at Kerry as they walked past. The shop assistant manning the till, leaned over her counter and looked at the sleeping Molly.

"Oh, what lovely hair she has," the woman exclaimed looking at the blond hair that framed Molly's face like a halo.

"Thank you," replied Kerry smugly as she stowed her purchases under the pram, "she got that from her father."

They were nearly home when they met Julie from the mother and baby group. An unavoidable encounter as they approached each other from opposite directions on the same side of the street.

"Hi, Kerry," Julie said. "Great to see you. Haven't seen you in ages. Why haven't you been coming to the group?"

"Oh, I've just been a bit under the weather, touch of flu, that's all, and I didn't want to spread my germs around you lot." Kerry gave the excuse she had rehearsed for such an occasion.

"Oh, poor you. I hope Molly didn't get it?"

"Just a case of the snuffles, but she'll be alright."

"Did you take her to the doctor?" Julie said and before Kerry could stop her, the woman had leant into the pram.

"Ah, there she is, Molly and her lovely hair. She must be sound asleep."

"Yes, we, um had a bad night, that's why, I expect." Excuse number two was forced between Kerry's lips.

"Mmm, she does look at bit pale." Julie was still leaning over the pram and Kerry didn't know what to do to stop her.

"She seems a bit small, Kerry, my Tyler has grown quite a bit in comparison."

"Yes, well, as I said, we've not been too well. I expect that's all it is. Now, sorry, but I'd like to get back home," and Kerry started to push the pram forwards, making Julie step smartly backwards out of the way.

"See you soon, I hope," Julie called, but Kerry didn't bother to reply, just continued to walk smartly away towards the sanctuary of her flat and, of course, Alan, who would be waiting for her and would worry if she was gone too long.

Julie watched Kerry walk away and wondered if everything was alright with her friend. Kerry had seemed stiff, unfriendly even, which was unlike her. Julie had been about to ask Kerry if she wanted to have a coffee with her, but it seemed Kerry couldn't wait to get away. Julie would have appreciated the company and found it hard to stop her emotional reaction to the rejection. She decided to have a coffee on her own and pushed the baby's pram into the café, catching the door as it closed, so it wouldn't slam behind her and disturb the few occupants.

She was glad of the hot milky brew put in front of her and answered the owner's friendly questions in monosyllables to make him go away and leave her alone. She looked down at Tyler, who was asleep in her buggy, parked by the side of the table and then wrapped her hands around the side of the mug. Looking into the swirling brew, a mixture of instant coffee and hot milk, she heard once again Bob's outraged reaction to her find in the metal cabinet. She knew he could be forceful, but had never before been on the receiving end of a tirade of shouts and expletives. It was as if he was yelling at one of his soldiers who had made a monumental cock up, instead of talking to his wife. He'd told her to keep her nose out of things that didn't concern her and to stop snooping in the garage. She had tried to tell him she wasn't snooping, just going for a new bulb. Why would going into her own garage be snooping, she'd asked?

He'd replied that it was snooping when she was looking at something that didn't belong to her. He'd grabbed her keys out of the lock of the cabinet and deftly removed the one to the cabinet lock as well as the one to the garage door. There, he'd said, with satisfaction, now she couldn't go into places where she wasn't wanted.

When Julie had asked what the white powder was, she'd realised she'd made a huge mistake. She'd pushed him too far as he'd gone as white as his bloody drugs and then, shockingly, slapped her across the face. The force of the blow had sent her sprawling across the floor of the garage. His hand had caught not just her cheek, but her ear as well, for he had big hands and as she lay on the floor, it buzzed, sounding just like the hum of the fridge in the kitchen.

Instead of being conciliatory after what he'd done, which is what Julie had expected, Bob was cold and quiet. She'd envisaged he would have been as shocked as she was at his overreaction to her find and immediately fall to the floor, showering her with kisses and begging for her forgiveness. In place of her fantasy, she'd heard him, over the buzzing in her ear, repacking the package, thumping it back onto the shelf and then banging the metal door closed. He'd locked it and walked over to her. Pulling her roughly up off the floor he bundled her out of the garage and onto the drive. Letting her go, he pulled down and locked the garage door. Unable to move because of the shock, Julie had just stood there like a marionette, waiting for him to pull her strings. He'd then dragged her off the drive and pushed her through the open front door, slamming it behind her. After she'd heard the car start and then drive away she'd stumbled to the mirror. As the sight of her red cheek confronted her, she'd been unable to stop the tears.

Since then, they'd barely spoken to each other. The only other time they'd had a conversation was when he'd threatened her. Told her to keep her mouth shut if she knew what was good for her. Described what would happen to her or Tyler if she even thought about telling anyone what she'd seen in the garage that night. On one level it was all a bit corny, his behaviour, his outrage and his violence. As though he were one of the Mitchell brothers acting out a scene from East Enders. But on another level Julie was sensible enough to know that his behaviour wasn't acceptable. He seemed to have turned from a committed soldier into a villain overnight. From a loving husband into a complete prick. He said he was doing it for the good of the family, so all she had to do was shut up and put up and everything would be alright.

Taking a sip of her drink, Julie wondered what on earth she should do. Bob dealing in drugs was the last thing she'd expected of him. He'd always been so law abiding and she couldn't begin to understand why he'd turned into a criminal. No doubt everyone needed more money than they had, but to do something like that - surely they weren't in such a bad financial state that he'd been desperate enough to turn to illegal activities to make a bit of money.

Such a thing was contrary to everything she believed in. Against the way she had been brought up. She'd been told over and over again by her parents - always do the right thing, even if you don't want to. Live by your own moral code and treat others as you would wish to be treated yourself. Well, a slap in the face was definitely not the way she wanted to be treated. And being a party to drug smuggling was abhorrent to her.

Julie wondered what her options were, as she drank the last of the coffee. She could go to the military police, the local police, welfare, or the Padre even. She knew she must do the right thing and tell someone in authority. The question was who should she speak to and when would she get the opportunity? Bob had taken to checking up on her by ringing at various times of the day, or calling in at home on some pretext or other. He'd refused to let her have the car so she could do some shopping and was staying in every night, sitting sullen and withdrawn beside her, in front of the television, brazenly going through her mobile phone, checking who she'd been talking to.

As she put down the mug, she tried to remember where she'd put that welfare leaflet. The one they'd got when they moved in, that gave the locations and telephone numbers of all the various departments and barracks on the Garrison. She could follow the advice in the leaflet and call the appropriate department. But the thought of what Bob would do to her if he was arrested and then let out on bail or something, frightened the shit out of her. As she grabbed her bag and stood up to go, still undecided about what to do, her mobile rang. Fishing it out of her bag, she saw the caller was Bob and she pushed the accept button, all thoughts of ringing the police pushed away by her fear of him.

17

"Right, boss," Billy said as he walked into Crane's office, a piece of paper in his hands. "This is a list of those soldiers here on Aldershot Garrison who have had paternity leave or compassionate leave in the last four months."

Billy handed the list over to Crane.

"Seems a bit small," Crane turned the paper over in his hand as if expecting there to be something on the back.

"Mustn't be the season, or something, I guess. Aren't more babies born nine months after a cold spell, as people go to bed to keep warm?" Billy's accompanying laugh was cut short by Crane's look and he mumbled, "Sorry, boss."

"What about the other Garrisons?" he asked, as Billy sat down in the chair next to Crane's desk.

"Yep, we've got some there too, so I've sent those lists to the local boys to check out. Should get the results of their enquiries in a couple of days."

"Oh well, it's only a case of checking that the women still have a child, so it shouldn't take long."

"Shall I just ring them, boss?"

"No, Billy. Think about it. What could happen if we ring?"

"Oh, sorry, the woman or the squaddie could lie."

"Exactly. Now piss off and put that list of names and addresses in some sort of reasonable driving order, so we're not zigzagging all over the Garrison and the town."

"Yes, boss. When do you want to start the door knocking?"

"Tomorrow morning will be soon enough. We'll start first thing."

Billy nodded and made to leave the office.

"Oh, Billy,"

"Sir?"

"Have you got your report ready on Wainwright? The one detailing your surveillance, with all the pictures and video clips attached?"

"Just finishing it off now, boss."

"Good, send it over as soon as, so I can pass it onto Captain Draper."

As Billy left the office, Crane turned to the list in his hand. There were 20 names on it. A fairly representative figure, he guessed, of young men becoming fathers from the whole of Aldershot Garrison. The list detailed their rank, current addresses and telephone numbers, but precious little else. What else was there to ask?

Crane wandered out into the car park outside Provost Barracks and lit a cigarette, all the time studying the list. Looking more closely at it, he realised the information also included date of birth, rank and service number of each soldier. Glancing down the list, most of the fathers were young men of lower rank with only three being officers. There was still something niggling him. What else did he need to know? What didn't the list show?

There had been a rain shower earlier that morning and Crane inadvertently splashed in a puddle, swearing as he wet his shoe, sock and the bottom of his trousers. Trying to shake the water from his trouser leg, he berated himself for the silly accident.

As he drew deeply on his cigarette, he realised the obvious information missing was the lads' Army records. Had any of them had discipline problems, or anger management problems? Those types of problems may be an indication of emotional instability, or a hint that they could have difficulty dealing with suddenly becoming a father, shortly after being married. And that may have led to an accident, a mishandling of the baby, or shaking it in anger or frustration. As Crane wandered around the car park, he remembered that there was nothing in the child's post mortem to indicate a traumatic death. But reasoning that perhaps something may have been overlooked, or not shown up at the time of the autopsy, such as bruising, then it may be an avenue worth pursuing.

Walking back into the SIB office, he made sure Sue had a copy of the list and he asked her to pull the Army records for each man on it. He then went to get his coat. There was someone he needed to speak to over a cup of coffee.

Crane arrived at the Garrison Church and creaked open the large wooden door. The interior was empty. The standards lining the nave looked like sentries and fluttered in the breeze as Crane opened and closed the door. Crane knew the way to the Padre's office, but if he hadn't he would have simply had to follow the enticing aroma of Arabica beans. As the Padre had become more and more involved with welfare matters for the various regiments stationed on the Garrison at any one time, his coffee percolator had become more and more popular. Crane walked to the back of the church and made his way through the gloom of the large stone building, to the office, looking over his shoulder as the ghosts of previous investigations seemed to follow him and he hurried through the cold corridor towards the bright lights shining through the open office door.

Crane knocked and at the Padre's call, entered the room. The stone walls would have presented a cold, unwelcoming interior, but bright lights chased the shadows into the corners and a new area boasting a colourful rug between two comfy chairs, with the coffee machine on a low table nearby, transformed the space.

"Good morning, Captain Symmonds," Crane said. "Do you have a minute?"

"Certainly, Crane, come in. I expect you want coffee?"

The Captain fussed over his machine and handed Crane a welcome black coffee. Once they were seated he wanted to know how he could help.

Crane handed the Padre a copy of the list of men who had taken paternity or compassionate leave recently and explained they were using this as a starting point for their investigation into the identity of the dead baby. Crane and Billy intended to interview the soldier or their wife or partner to see if all was well and they still had their child.

"Fair enough," said Padre Symmonds. "So what do you want from me?" he asked, putting the list down on the table without looking at it.

"I wondered if you would look through the list and

see if any of those soldiers came for welfare support. Maybe they had a marital problem, or problems with fatherhood, that sort of thing."

"Are you forgetting that my sessions with them are confidential?"

"Not at all, sir," said Crane, placing his mug on the low table. "I just want to know if anyone of them had come with any relevant problems. If you could just indicate if there are any names on the list that you are familiar with, that would help."

"In what way?"

"We may then look more closely at those soldiers."

"Crane, if someone has had leave, then they are bound to have a child."

"Not necessarily, sir, they could have had compassionate leave for another reason. Not every Regiment records leave in the same way. Nor do they keep track of how many children a soldier has. So…."

"I see what you mean," the Padre took a swallow of coffee before continuing. "One of these soldiers could have had a child, but it died. If so, conceivably, it could be the one we found left at the church. However, if there is nothing on their service record to indicate fatherhood, they could simply deny ever having a child. Oh dear." The Captain looked into his coffee mug, then put it down on the table and pushed it away from him. "Wouldn't the birth be registered?"

"It should be," said Crane, "but it's a lot of work for us to check up on each soldier initially through the Birth Deaths and Marriages Registrar. So I want to whittle the list down first. Then we could look more closely at any suspicious family."

"Yes, I see." The Padre put his elbows on his knees and his hands under his chin. After a ponderous moment during which Crane worried at the scar under his beard, Captain Symmonds said, "Very well, Crane, let me have a look at the list. I'll not give you any reasons why I know any of the soldiers, mind. Just indicate, informally you understand, that a certain soldier may be worth talking to."

Crane tried hard not to break into a grin at the Padre's words and managed a sober, "Thank you, sir. Do you want me to leave the list with you?"

"No, I'll do it now, while you enjoy your coffee."

Crane didn't have to wait very long, as the Padre only knew two of the men on the list. But it was his next statement that Crane found very interesting.

"I know of one other family that aren't on this list. A young soldier was killed in Afghanistan and the story goes that when his wife got the news, the shock caused her to go into labour, right there on the doorstep. I remember some of the lads telling me about it at his funeral. Now what was the soldier's name? Just a minute, Crane," and the Padre jumped up and went to his desk. Pulling out his diary he checked some dates.

"Here we are," the Padre carried the diary back to his armchair. "I've got his funeral recorded in the diary. The soldier was called Chandler, Alan Chandler."

Disappointment

Kerry awoke to silence. From her prone position on the small single bed, she turned her head and looked at the cot and listened. Nothing. No cry, no snuffling, no squirming. Sighing, she pushed away the duvet, swung her legs out of bed and pushed her feet into her backless slippers. She stood and looked into Molly's cot. She was lying on her front, legs and arms down and her face turned sideways. In exactly the same position as when Kerry put her to bed last night and carefully covered her with her favourite blanket.

Kerry grabbed her dressing gown off the bottom of the bed and shrugged her way into it. Slapping her way out of the room, she left the baby where she was and went into the kitchen to put the kettle on for a mug of tea. The flat was so quiet that she jumped at the sound of the boiler turning itself on to warm the water for the radiators.

She glanced over at Alan, who was sitting in his chair. Motionless. Silent. His opaque eyes seeing nothing. His mouth frozen open. His eyebrows high in terror. She expected he was constantly reliving the explosion. Well who wouldn't? It wouldn't be something you'd forget easily, she imagined. But she'd thought he'd have come to terms with it by now, even just a little bit. After all these months. At least enough for his face to relax. But it seemed not.

He didn't move much either. I don't know, she thought, they're much the same, Molly and her husband. Both frozen in time and place. They were not only finding it hard to move, but also finding it hard to communicate with her - and she with them sometimes.

After she'd made her tea, she took it over to the settee and turned on the television, flicking through the channels to find something of interest. Eventually she settled on Daybreak, it being more gossipy and celebrity driven than the more formal news stuff on the other channels. She'd had enough horror in her own life, without hearing about other peoples'.

She was so used to no one speaking to her the majority of the time, that she jumped when Alan interrupted a particularly interesting piece on fashion that she was watching. Not that she had much money for new outfits, but it was nice to see what the rest of the world was wearing, so she snapped at him in annoyance.

"What? What did you say?" she grumbled over her shoulder. "Where's Molly? Where do you think she is? She's in her cot." She turned to look at him and listened for a moment. "No, she's not making any noise is she," she replied. "She never makes any bloody noise. It's all very well for her to be a big comfort to me. For me to have a baby to hold in my arms again, but, well, I just wish… I wish she'd **do** more, you know?"

By now Alan had completely interrupted the piece on fashion, so she gave him her full attention. After all she did want him to stay around and he might go away if she wasn't nice to him. So she listened intently to what he had to say next.

"Get another one?" she asked. After a moment's thought she continued, "You know, you could have a point there, Alan. Because the thing is Molly isn't growing. That Julie I told you about, well she said Molly was a bit small for her age. Well she would be, this Molly is only three months old and our Molly would be nearer five by now. Babies grow a lot in that time. I tell you what, I'll just have my tea, then go and take a look on the computer. I think I remember seeing that you could get the babies tailored to your own needs, so I'll give it a go. Not that I want to get rid of this Molly, Alan. I do love her, I just want her to do a bit more, cry, laugh, chuckle, anything would be good, you know?"

Alan told her he understood and he was sure his clever wife could sort something out. She preened under his praise and rushed over to turn the computer on. Bugger getting dressed, she thought, she could do that later.

18

The door of Kerry Chandler's apartment was a cheery red, incongruous within the context of the mainly concrete structure. As Crane looked along the landing, he saw the doors of the other dwellings were painted in equally bright colours. The apartments were on one side of the landing and on the other a bright blue railing had been constructed atop the concrete wall, whether for show or to stop inebriated residents falling to their deaths, Crane wasn't sure. The whole block had a rugged industrial feel to it, a sort of urban chic, that it didn't quite pull off, for on closer inspection the front doors were chipped and scuffed and the railings going rusty on the underside.

Billy knocked on the door of flat 6B. A muffled voice called, "Just a minute," accompanied by mumbles and the clatter of dishes. When no-one had opened the door after a minute or so, Billy knocked again, louder and shouted "Mrs Chandler, Royal Military Police here, can we have a word?"

After much fumbling and turning of locks, the door was opened on a secure chain and a pale, freckled female face looked through the slit.

Crane and Billy held up their identification badges, which they wore around their necks.

"Mrs Kerry Chandler?" Crane enquired.

The woman nodded her head several times but didn't speak.

"Sgt Major Crane and Sgt Williams from the Branch on Aldershot Garrison. Can we come in please?"

His question was considered, then after more nodding of her head, Kerry opened the door and let them in.

As Crane stepped inside with Billy, they were immediately in a small living area. He could see two doors on one side of the room, both of which were open. One revealed a small kitchen, whose work surfaces were covered with packages of food and dirty dishes and the other a small bathroom. That had a linen basket on view, which was overflowing with dirty clothes. Towels were strewn over the floor as if there had been a leak and they'd been used to soak up the water. The door on the opposite wall was also open, showing an unmade bed and just the corner of what looked like it could be a wooden cot.

"Sorry to disturb you, Mrs Chandler, we just wondered if we could talk to you for a few minutes."

"Yes, um, yes, why don't you sit down and please, call me Kerry."

Crane looked uncertainly at the shabby lumpy settee, but decided to risk it as Billy sat beside him and Kerry sat down gingerly on the armchair opposite them.

"Kerry, do you know that a baby was left at the Garrison Church a few weeks ago?"

"Um, yes, I read about it in the paper."

Kerry was perched right on the front of her chair and seemed to be squirming to get comfortable, but

Crane couldn't see that she'd sat on anything other than the chair seat.

"Well, we're contacting all Army personnel who have a baby about that age, such as yourself."

"Army personnel?" Kerry's question came out as a squeak. Clearing her throat, she continued, "I'm not Army personnel. I stopped having anything to do with the Army the day my husband died."

Crane saw that talking about the Army changed the young woman's demeanour from mouse to lion so quickly, he thought he might have imagined it. But no, he could see the anger in the flashing of her green eyes and the stiffening of her red-haired head.

"So I really don't think you have any authority here, do you?" she finished.

"Please, Kerry, we're very sorry for your loss," Crane looked at Billy who nodded his agreement. "We just wanted to ask if you knew of any mothers who had a child and now don't. We just want to trace the parents of the poor baby that was left at the church and help them, that's all."

"Oh, sorry. It's just that the Army's a bit of a sore point, you know?"

His conciliatory words had seemed to mollify the woman, but Crane decided to take a different tack with his questions, rather than antagonise her further. Her mood changes were rather alarming.

"How long have you lived here, Kerry?"

"Oh, a few months now. The council got me this place."

"Yes, I thought they would have done. It's a good flat," he said looking around.

"Thank you. It's a good job I'd just done the housework before you arrived," she said. "I wouldn't have wanted you to think I lived in a mess."

Crane thought that a very strange comment, as the flat was unspeakably muddled and very definitely not clean. At least not by his standards. But then he knew civilians didn't have the same standards as soldiers. A fact pointed out to him by his wife, many times over the course of their marriage.

"You just said, I, Kerry," Billy pointed out. "Don't you mean *we* lived in a mess? You do have a baby don't you?"

Kerry blushed, a fiery red stain spreading upwards from her neck all the way to her sculpted cheek bones. She tossed her mane of ginger curls and said, "Of course I do, she's called Molly."

Deliberately grinning, feeling like a crocodile smiling a false smile, Crane said, "What a lovely name. May we see her?"

"See her?" Kerry echoed and started plucking at the jumper she was wearing over leggings. Her feet were bare and as her legs were crossed, she was swinging one of them.

"Yes, I'd love to see her," said Crane "I've a boy just coming up to one year old and I love seeing other people's children. They're all so different aren't they?" Crane stood. "In the bedroom is she?" he asked and walked over to the door, standing half in and half out of the room. "Ah, yes," he called. "She must be sound asleep, she's not even moving. Come and look, Billy," and Crane used calling for Billy as an excuse to move further into the room.

Molly was lying on her front, her head turned sideways away from him, towards the wall. He could just see a pink cheek and curly blond hair that spilled onto the pillow. Her arms were outstretched and she had dainty little hands with perfect miniature nails on them.

Crane nodded to Billy and they both left the bedroom and walked towards the flat door.

"She really is beautiful, Kerry."

"Thank you," she said.

"Well, we'll be off now and if you do think of anyone whose baby may have died, give me a ring would you? Remember, we only want to help," and he handed Kerry a card with his name and telephone numbers on and then opened the front door. As they stepped out onto the landing, the door was immediately pushed closed behind them.

Crane and Billy looked at each other, but didn't speak until they were back at their car.

"W-ie-rd," said Billy.

"I definitely think she has some issues," said Crane. "Mind you, who wouldn't in her situation?"

"That flat smelled disgusting," Billy wrinkled his nose at the memory. "Did she really think it was clean?"

"Buggered if I know. If so, it could just be a reflection of her distraught emotional state at the moment. Still, at least she had a baby. Mind you, I didn't see her move."

"Move?"

"Yes. Daniel can't seem to keep still sometimes when he sleeps. Always snuffling, or shuffling. Molly seemed unnaturally still by comparison."

"I wouldn't know about that, boss, being footloose and fancy free myself. But there's not much else we can do. She has a baby and that's that."

As they got in the car and drove to the next address on their list, something was bugging Crane. Poking at his brain, but just out of recollection. As he pulled up outside the next soldier's quarter, he had it. He turned to Billy and said, "Don't you think Molly looked remarkably like the dead baby we found?"

Molly #2

At last the second doll had arrived. Kerry had spent the past few days anxiously looking out of the window, watching for the delivery van. In fact she had been altogether rather anxious since the visit by the two men from the Branch. She didn't know much about the Branch, only that Alan always said they were the ones who investigated the more serious crimes. She guessed leaving a dead baby in the church doorway counted as something quite serious. But she'd managed to get through the interview. She thought she'd done rather well, actually. Although Alan wasn't at all impressed with being sat on. But as she'd explained to him, she couldn't very well stand when there was what appeared to be an empty chair in the room. Anyway all that was behind her now. She was sure they'd leave her alone after seeing Molly in her cot.

At last the time for the grand unwrapping had come. Kerry put Molly in her highchair and pulled it next to the settee, so she could watch as well as Alan, who was sitting in his armchair as usual. Both of them eying Kerry keenly while she undid the package. Molly was very excited about having a sister. As she worked, Kerry explained to her that it wasn't that mummy didn't love her anymore, it was just that, just that (Kerry stumbled a bit over this part of the explanation) it was just that her sister would be able to do more things than Molly could. It was all part of growing up, she explained. As babies get older, they are able to do more. Molly appeared satisfied with that and so Kerry got on with opening the box.

As she revealed the reborn to her expectant family, Kerry experienced a huge surge of pride. She might not come from a very good social background and she had to admit that her and her mum had been very poor. But she had learned a lot from her mother, especially about how not to treat children. And it was because of that bad start in life that she was now excelling at looking after her own family - even if she did say so herself.

Kerry lifted the baby out of her box, reverently. Holding her as though she were made of porcelain. A collective gasp filled the room. The baby was absolutely beautiful. She had Molly's blond hair (Kerry had decided this should be a family trait out of respect for Alan and Molly) peeking out of a small woollen cap. She was weighted just like Molly, but this time her head didn't need extra support, the new baby being that bit older and a whole two inches longer. Dressed in adorable pink PJ's decorated with little white fluffy dogs, she was able to sit up on Kerry's knee. Her blue eyes, framed by dark eyelashes, were wide in amazement at the first sight of her new family and she seemed about to chuckle with happiness. You could even see her tiny pink tongue through her open mouth and a couple of teeth were poking out of her bottom gum. Kerry was glad about that, not wanting to have too much trouble with teething.

Kerry had prepared for the new baby girl and had batteries to hand, under the coffee table. Turning the baby onto her front and un-popping her sleep suit, Kerry inserted the batteries and redressed the child. Turning her back over, Kerry laid her along her knees and put her finger to the tiny hand, holding her breath, waiting for the child to respond. And then it happened. It was truly a miracle, just like the advert had said. The child curled her hand around Kerry's finger!

"Oh my God, Alan, look, look what she's just done," Kerry gabbled and quickly removed her finger, only to see the child's hand open again. "She can grab my finger, she can, Alan, look, look I tell you," and Kerry repeated the movement so Alan could watch the baby grasp her finger.

Holding the child over her shoulder, she leaned her ear to the tiny chest. She felt the gentle up and down movements of the little one's rib cage as the child breathed in and out, in and out, in and out. Kerry became mesmerized. Holding a child that breathed, grabbed her finger and smelled so sweetly of talcum powder was almost more than she could bear. It brought the memories of holding Molly when she was first born rushing back in a torrent of emotion that she couldn't contain. Her tears spilled unhindered down her cheeks. This time her daughter truly had been returned to her, she was sure of it.

It was Alan's cough that brought her back from those precious memories. Kerry manoeuvred the little one round until she was sitting on her knee. As the new baby was looking around at Alan and Molly, Kerry supported her with one hand and with the other rooted through the packaging. Her hand closed over a piece of paper and she pulled it out, thinking it would just be a delivery note. But it was something far more exciting.

"Look, Alan, it's a Birth Certificate, all ready for us to fill in. Here, you have your first cuddle with her while I get a pen."

The new baby fitted into the crook of Alan's arm, as though she had always meant to be there. Kerry knew that he was hurting too and needed to be healed by the baby's touch, as she had just been. Realising that the two of them needed to be left alone for a moment, to bond, she turned away and went into the kitchen. Rummaging through the kitchen drawers she found a pen. "Got one," she called as she ran back into the sitting room. "Right, we first have to decide on a name."

She looked expectantly at Alan and then Molly, but didn't get a reply.

"Come on, you two," she said. "One of you must have an idea. Oh well, I'll give you a few moments to think, while I fill in the rest of the form. First of all the names of the parents, well that part is easy. Father, Alan Chandler, occupation, soldier. Mother, Kerry Chandler, occupation, housewife."

Kerry went on to fill in the rest of the certificate. Finishing, she set down her pen and looked at Alan, Molly and the un-named baby.

"So, what do you think? What shall we call her? Chrissie? Summer? Lucy?"

Kerry rattled off a few more names, but it was Alan who explained it in the end. He said the new baby had to be called Molly as well, otherwise what would happen when Kerry went out and people saw her. She couldn't very well introduce another baby, could she? No, they should be called Molly #1 and Molly #2.

"Oh, Alan," Kerry rushed over to kiss him. "You're

so clever. Come on then Molly #2, let me show you around," and she took the baby from Alan and walked around the flat, showing Molly #2 her new home.

Crawling

Kerry was in the middle of a huge row with Alan. It didn't happen very often, as she was very careful not to upset him in case he went away. But this time it was different. She couldn't contain all the hurt, anger and loss anymore. He needed to know how she really felt.

It had all started when she'd seen Julie the previous day. Kerry had some grocery shopping to do, so she'd walked to the shops in North Camp. They'd stopped to chat, although Kerry was always wary of people looking too closely at Molly #2 in the pram, but she couldn't get rid of Julie yesterday morning. The bloody woman just wouldn't stop talking. She cooed about the babies, as one would expect, but she also insisted on talking about her husband.

Bob this, it was and Bob that, she went on. A bit bloody insensitive on Julie's part, Kerry thought, as Julie still had her husband and Alan had been blown to bits. Anyway Julie hadn't seemed very happy. Apparently Bob kept going out at all hours of the day and night. Trying to tell her it was work and he couldn't help it. Work, my arse, was Julie's opinion. It was rather frightening what he was actually up to, she'd confided.

Although she wouldn't come out and say what it was that he was doing. She'd just kept hinting that it wasn't altogether legal. She'd also said that he didn't take much notice of their child, Tyler. That seemed to be particularly upsetting to Julie, as Tyler was crawling now, if you please! Soon she'd be taking her first steps, well doesn't time fly with babies, and Julie desperately wanted Bob to be involved with the girl and be as intoxicated by her as she was.

Julie had then twittered on about how nice it was to have someone to talk to. Someone to tell her troubles to. Someone who wasn't bound by the Army way anymore. She'd not been able to tell anyone on the Garrison that she was having marital problems, she'd said, because Bob had already given her a lecture on that. The gossip would go round and round their circle of friends (and even get to the ears of those who weren't in their circle) and find its way back to him. Then she'd be told off for talking about their problems, for letting others think their marriage wasn't working. According to Julie, Bob had said that he was a bloody Sergeant for goodness sake and what did Julie think would happen if any gossip about him or his wife got around the lower ranks? He'd lose face, that's what. Lose his standing in the eyes of his men. Lose their respect. They might not obey his orders or respect his judgement and then the whole thing would go to hell in a handbag. Heaven forbid that should happen, Julie had commented dryly. It was as though Bob thought the heavens would fall in around their heads and they would lose everything, just because of some idle chit chat.

Kerry had thought it was all rather over the top. And by then she was so pissed off with Julie that she'd actually told her so. The words spewing out of her mouth before she could stop them. That had shut Julie up. Made her think. Made her realise. Made her apologise for stupidly going on and on about her husband when Kerry's husband Alan had given his life for his country. Julie had begged for Kerry's forgiveness. Kerry had only just about managed to nod stiffly to acknowledge the apology, before she walked away, leaving Julie standing next to her own pram, open mouthed.

She'd been telling Alan all about this. But what had upset Kerry the most wasn't the fact that Julie's husband was still alive, but that her baby was crawling.

"It's all very well you saying I should be thankful that I've got Molly #1 in her high chair and Molly #2 in her baby bouncer, but what I should have, by rights, is Molly #3, crawling all over the carpet and starting to hold onto things to pull herself up."

"What right?" asked Alan. "What gives you the right to have Molly #3?"

"Because I'm a bloody good mother, that's why, Alan," she screamed at him. "I deserve it, I've been through enough. I've had enough of this shitty life. I want the same life as everyone else!"

"Oh, so it's shitty, is it?" Alan said. "Well thank you very much for that. I'm doing my best, staying here with you, instead of being somewhere nice and warm, peaceful and serene, like Heaven for instance."

"All I want is a baby that crawls and walks and talks," she screamed at him. "What's so bad about that? Why is that too much to ask? Why, Alan? Why?" Kerry sobbed, losing control. Tears streaked her face. Her hair was damp with sweat, making the curls stick wildly out. Her chest heaved as she tried to suck in air and her nose was running most unattractively.

Kerry ran into the bedroom, away from the mocking stares of the two Mollies and away from Alan's opaque eyes. The eyes he couldn't use to see how upset she was, how lonely she was, how tired she was from trying to make the best of things. She just couldn't do it anymore. She flung herself face down on the bed and sobbed until she fell asleep from sheer exhaustion.

19

Julie Wainwright was still very upset about Bob's drug smuggling. As she walked over to the shops in North Camp, pushing Tyler in her buggy, she thought about her encounter with Kerry the other day. When she'd seen Kerry, she hadn't been able to stop pouring out her hurt over her husband, completely forgetting that Kerry was now a widow. Julie hadn't actually told Kerry that Bob was dealing in drugs, although it had been hard not to. She'd just hinted at his bad behaviour. She'd been desperate for someone to talk to. Someone who would understand the strain she was under. Understand the dilemma she was in. Understand her inability to make a decision. The decision about whether or not she should tell the police about Bob's illegal activities.

The trouble was she knew that if Bob was caught, then it would be her who would lose everything, as well as him. He would be thrown out of the Army and sent to military prison and then probably civilian prison after that. As a result she'd lose her home, her way of life, her friends and Bob's salary - never mind his pension. So it wasn't just Bob's threats of violence that were stopping her, it was the threat to Tyler's future.

Plus she'd seen what Kerry looked like. Pale and wan, a shadow of her former self. Julie remembered Kerry as a lively, outgoing person, who would do anything for her friends. But that was when Alan was still alive and the baby hadn't been born. The shock of the loss of her husband, her way of life, her house and her friends was clear in every line on Kerry's young face, making her look so much older than she was. There were bruises of tiredness under her eyes and the wild look in them was mirrored by her hair, which stuck straight out from her head in an angry ginger afro.

Julie had to walk to the shops that morning, because Bob was still taking the car with him to work every day and in her present state, she couldn't face taking the bus into Aldershot or Farnborough, so she'd decided to walk up the road to get a few bits of shopping. She'd written a list of what she wanted and drifted up and down the aisles of the local Co-op, list in one hand, pushing the buggy with the other, pretty much oblivious to everyone and everything, including the piped music that followed her along the aisles. Her head was full of her marital problems.

As she stood in the queue to pay, she watched people's shopping being pulled along on the conveyor belt and then disappearing into carrier bags. She wished she could do that to her problems. Make them disappear. Out of sight, out of mind. She hadn't been brave enough to ask Bob if the drugs were still in the garage and was hoping to God that if they were still there, they'd be gone soon. She guessed she'd know when they had been sold on as Bob would suddenly have money. She just hoped he'd pay the bills with it and not blow it on unnecessary luxury items.

Coming out of the shop she was still thinking about how nice it would be, though, to have a bit of money put by. Take the strain off the monthly budget, pay off the credit cards for instance, so lowering the amount they had to pay out every month. She had to admit that with a growing baby the cost of nappies and new clothes, not to mention shoes when Tyler started walking, was beginning to worry her. She'd been thinking she might have to go back to work. But if Bob did sell the drugs, maybe she wouldn't have to.

The ringing of her mobile interrupted her thoughts and digging it out of her pocket, she saw it was Bob calling her.

Swallowing back her nervousness, she answered his call.

"Julie? Where the hell are you?" he shouted.

"What?" she stammered. "I'm, I'm just at the shops in North Camp."

"Well you should bloody well be at home. I've come back to have some lunch with you and you're not here and I can't find anything to eat."

"Sorry, I'll be back in a few minutes."

"Make sure you bring something for me to have for lunch, then."

"Oh, right, yes, how about a hot Cornish pasty? I'm right outside the bakers."

"Make it two," he said and disconnected the call.

Julie looked at the phone and with shaking hands slipped it back into her pocket. Looking through the small square panes of glass into the shop, she was relieved to see pasties in the hot cabinet. She pushed her handbag further up onto her shoulder and walked in to the bakery, focused on buying Bob some lunch and then getting home as quickly as she could.

Fall Out

Kerry was also walking up and down the streets of North Camp. She felt cut off from society, adrift in her sea of grief, without a lifejacket. Not wanting to be cooped up in the flat anymore, she'd gone out, without any particular destination in mind. All on her own. No Molly #1, nor Molly #2. She was fed up with them both. Fed up and angry because they weren't able to do what she wanted them to do. What she needed them to do. Fed up because they weren't as clever, as happy or as real as bloody Julie Wainwright's baby, Tyler.

She recognised she was experiencing some sort of fallout from the row with Alan a few days ago. It was as though there had been some sort of nuclear reaction at the explosion of her anger. After her bombshell when she'd told him that she didn't like her life. The contaminated particles had fallen down around her in the flat. Coating Alan, so she couldn't see him anymore. Covering the Mollies, so she couldn't feel their love anymore. Unable to bear the loneliness, she had been driven out onto the streets, hoping for some human contact.

But there was no release for her out on the streets

either. Everything and everyone seemed to shimmer before her eyes, as though she were viewing life from the other side of a piece of frosted glass. She could hear the cars as they manoeuvred their way around the narrow streets, following the one way system faithfully, gears crashing and horns hooting. She watched the elderly pick their way carefully along the cobbled pavements, jumping at any unexpected loud noise. She looked through the shop windows at the customers in the queues, impatiently waiting to pay for their purchases.

She walked around the supermarket, not bothering to take a basket for she didn't want to buy anything. She smiled at the cashiers, working away like beavers, constantly reaching and scanning, reaching and scanning, reaching and scanning. She tried to catch the eye of the nearest worker, but the woman looked at Kerry without seeing her, safe behind her counter, safe where she belonged. It was the same with everyone she walked past. No one looked her in the eye, smiled at her, or even scowled at her. She seemed invisible.

Kerry wandered back out onto the street, wondering how she could break through the invisible shield surrounding her and become a normal woman again. She didn't seem to have the tools anymore. The life skills. It had been so long since she'd really talked to anyone, had a proper meaningful conversation with someone, that she was afraid she'd forgotten how to communicate with the living. Her world consisted of the dead now, but even they'd let her down. She sat down on a bench in the sun, closed her eyes and tried looking at her life from Alan and Molly's point of view. Maybe that was it. Maybe that's what Alan and Molly wanted. Maybe it was time for her to go and be with them, become part of their life, rather than forcing them to be part of hers. She smiled at the thought. Her first real smile in ages.

Later, thinking back, she realised it must have been her smile that did it. The smile that shattered the glass which was shielding her from the world and brought her back from the brink. For at that very moment, she heard the piercing cry of a baby. It echoed around the street, bouncing off the broken shards that fell around her feet and in her wake, as she ran across the road.

She didn't have time for conscious thought. She just acted on her maternal instincts. She heard a child in distress and so went to comfort it. There was no one standing by the pram, no one reaching in to take the child in their arms, so Kerry did. She simply picked up the child, held it close to her body, wrapped her coat over it and walked away. The movement and closeness seemed to soothe the child and by the time Kerry got back to her flat, it was fast asleep.

20

Thank God, the shop had had some pasties left, was Julie's overriding thought as she came out of the bakery, juggling the hot package, her change, her purse and her handbag. She bent down and put the pasties under the buggy, then straightened so she could put her change away. She dumped her handbag down on the seat of the buggy and opened her purse. Then stood still. She looked down at her handbag again. To all intents and purposes she'd just plonked her handbag on top of Tyler. But that wasn't the case. For Tyler wasn't in her buggy.

Julie picked up the offending bag to make sure. But the child still wasn't there. She stood immobile outside the shop, holding her purse in one hand and her bag in the other. Her confused brain trying to make sense of the unthinkable. She'd lost her baby. Tyler wasn't where she was supposed to be. She looked up and down the street, but couldn't see Tyler in anyone's arms. In fact there were very few people about. They were probably all at home having lunch, she thought. Where she should be. At home having lunch with Bob and Tyler.

She sank down onto the pavement next to the

buggy. Wondering what she should do? Wondering who would help? This couldn't be happening, she thought. Not to her, not today, not on a quiet street in North Camp. What the bloody hell was going on?

Julie became aware of someone coming out of the shop, taking hold of her arm and asking if she was alright. As she looked into the worried face of the shop assistant from the bakery and tried to make sense of the woman's words, she became aware of a scream. It seemed far away but heading in her direction, as if it was flying down the street towards her, getting louder and louder as it got closer and closer, until it slammed into her.

That's when she realised she was screaming and that she couldn't stop.

When Crane arrived at the scene in North Camp, everyone was as shocked and pale-faced as the mother who'd had her baby snatched. Anderson kept running his hands through his rapidly thinning hair as he explained to Crane what had happened and why he'd been called out.

"Jesus Christ," was Crane's reaction. "So, it's true. A baby has been snatched."

Anderson's confirming nod shattered his illusive hope that he'd been given the wrong information.

"And the parents are military?"

"Yes."

Crane took a moment to close his eyes and compose himself. Just because he was a soldier didn't mean he was hard as nails. Didn't mean he didn't have emotions. It just meant he was better at boxing them off than most people. But the loss of a young baby pierced the invisible shield he held around his heart. His overriding thought being, thank God it's not Daniel. Patching over the emotional wound, he returned his features to their usual stern arrangement and turned back to Derek.

"Where's the mother?"

"Over there, sat on the pavement outside the bakery. We can't get her to move, so her husband's trying to persuade her that she's got to get up and go with him. We've called out a WPC to act as family liaison and we need them to go home, as the WPC is going to meet them there - Crane, wait!" Anderson called, but Crane was already walking over to the couple.

As he approached them he watched the man, talking animatedly to his wife, looming over her as she sat on the curb.

"What the hell were you thinking of? How could you be so stupid?" Crane heard him say and watched as the soldier threw his arms in the air to make his point.

Not wanting to hear anymore, Crane called out to him, "Excuse me, sir, Sgt Major Crane from the Branch. Can I have a word?"

The father lowered his arms and turned to face Crane, who at that moment had his worst nightmare realised. For the father of the missing child was no other than Bob Wainwright, his main suspect in the drugs smuggling ring. Crane's ability to remain poker faced was severely challenged as he said, "Over here, please, sir," and he turned, leading the man back to Anderson. When his back was turned to Wainwright, Crane raised his eyebrows to Derek, his wide eyes saying a silent 'what the fuck?' to which Anderson shrugged in reply.

The three men moved to stand some way from Julie Wainwright.

"Sgt Wainwright," Anderson said, "we really need

you to get your wife home. We're doing all we can here and a family liaison officer will meet you at your house. Also a DC will be calling to ask you both more questions and we urgently need an up to date photo of Tyler."

"What questions? What good will more bloody questions do?" Wainwright's anger that they'd just seen him turn on his wife, was still bubbling just under the surface of his barely polite demeanour. Crane already didn't like the man because of his thieving, smuggling ways and now his distain of the so called soldier, increased. For as far as Crane was concerned, he could now add a bully and a coward to Wainwright's list of flaws.

"If we have a good idea of your wife's normal routine, places she goes to, mother and baby groups for instance, then we can see if there is a pattern where she might intersect with other people, or other mothers who may be able to help with our enquiries."

"So you want to forensically examine our life? Even though it might not help?"

"Well, you could put it that way, sir, but surely you want us to do everything we can to find Tyler? And a piece of information that seems trivial to you, sir, could be very illuminating to us."

Wainwright just stood glaring at them without speaking, until Crane said, "Sgt Wainwright, please take your wife home. Now." A growl.

Wainwright slowly turned to face Crane and for a moment the two looked at each other, oblivious to everyone else around them. But Crane outranked the Sergeant and they both knew it. So it was Wainwright who said, "Very well, sir," and moved away, going back to his wife, leaning down and whispering in her ear, before helping her, non too gently, to her feet.

Once Wainwright was out of earshot Crane said, "What the hell? Wainwright! What's the odds of that happening?"

"Multimillions to one, I'm sure," laughed Anderson.

"You may well laugh, Derek, but I'll have a lot of poker faces to wear during this investigation."

"Do you want Billy to be Army liaison on this one instead of you?"

"No, his poker face would lose him thousands of pounds in a casino. Anyway, what's next?"

"Right, we've got uniform going door to door through the shops on the street, forensics are on their way to go over the pram and a couple of DCs are grabbing any CCTV footage from local businesses. There's lads at the station on their way over to the CCTV Centre in Farnborough, which covers North Camp, to check their recordings."

"Good. I'll get Billy to look at the cameras on the Garrison to follow Julie Wainwright from her house, over to North Camp, just in case anyone was following her. What about the Press?" asked Crane.

"As soon as we've got that photograph, there'll be a press conference at the Station. In about an hour I should think."

"Okay I'll go back to Barracks and call Padre Symmonds and get him to go over to the Wainwright's house as well as your officer. Even if the Wainwright's don't want him to stay, we need to offer them support from the Army as well. Email the picture of the baby over to Billy as soon as you get it, would you? He can circulate it around the RMPs. Just in case Tyler has been taken by someone who lives on the Garrison. See you back at the police station to meet the press."

"Thanks, Crane," said Anderson and they parted to go back to their cars, neither man looking forward to the coming days, or possibly weeks. Crane knew it was bad enough dealing with a drugs ring, and the cat and mouse game they were playing, trying to stay one step ahead of their opposition. But when one of the suspects had just had a baby snatched, Crane knew it was impossible to predict what might happen next and that the ramifications any outcome in the kidnapping case, might have on the drug smuggling case, and vice versa.

21

Padre Symmonds was nothing short of flabbergasted when Crane rang him.

"A snatched baby?"

He'd said that twice already. Crane knew how he felt. Everyone at Provost Barracks had been just as horrified. Including Captain Draper. The trouble was they were all family men to a greater or lesser extent. Even those not married could find empathy with the devastated parents. What if it was their nephew or niece? Brother or sister? Those that were married had an overriding need to go home and gather their little ones in their arms. But they were on duty. So they stayed on duty. Unable to leave their Barracks. One of the many Army versus family struggles soldiers had to deal with every day of their service.

Crane gave the Padre the details of the parents and their address. But he didn't tell him Wainwright was suspected of drug smuggling. Strongly suspected. Although they hadn't been able to check that there were actually drugs in the ration boxes in his garage. They wouldn't know that for sure until the hand over to Josip Anic.

There was silence at the other end of the line, so Crane said, "Are you still there, Padre?"

"Oh, sorry, yes, Crane. I was just thinking about a dead baby left on the church steps and now a missing baby. Any connection do you think?"

"At the moment, we really don't have any idea, sir."

"Just wondering out loud, but, maybe the woman whose baby died, could have snatched a baby by way of compensating for her loss?"

"As I said, sir, at the moment, we have no idea."

"Very well, Crane, I'll take the hint, keep my nose out of your investigation and get on with my job of supporting the parents."

"Thank you, sir. Sorry, but you know the drill."

"Indeed I do," laughed the Padre, more sardonic than humorous, having been involved in more than one of Crane's investigations in the past. "Right, I'll get over there."

"One more thing, Padre."

"Yes, Crane?"

"If you hear anything which could help the investigation, please call me ASAP. Anything the parents say that could provide a link between the mother and the snatcher. You never know what they may say without thinking or realising, that could help."

After the slightest of hesitations, the Padre said, "Very well, Crane. Normally I would treat anything someone says to me during a welfare visit as confidential, but I feel these are, shall we say, extenuating circumstances. So if there's anything at all that I think you should know, or even if I don't know if it could help, I'll call straight away."

"Thank you, sir. I'm available anytime, day or night."

After replacing the receiver, Crane took a deep

breath and went to see Captain Draper. Not sure how his boss would work with him on a major investigation. Untried territory and all that.

"Come," was the call from Draper's office in response to Crane's knock.

"Afternoon, sir," Crane said as he entered.

"Ah, Crane, good, come to give me a report about the baby, have you?"

"Yes, sir," and Crane detailed the parts of the investigation underway to date.

"Okay," Draper leaned back in his chair. "Thoughts?"

Here we go, thought, Crane. I do all the work as usual. But he managed to push away his negativity and said, "Connections."

"Alright, what connections have we got?"

"Dead baby and missing baby. Garrison church. Army family. Those are the main ones. Oh and the drug smuggling, but I'm feeling that's completely separate."

"You don't think its Anic making sure Wainwright comes through with the drugs?"

"To be honest, boss, no," Crane fingered the scar under his beard, "but I'll run it passed DI Anderson. See if he thinks that's how Anic operates." Crane was pleasantly surprised. It made a pleasant change for an OC to offer suggestions rather than shouts.

"Good. Do they look anything alike, the two babies?"

"Don't know, sir, still waiting for the photo to come through from Anderson. But they're both female."

"Hmmm," Draper took a moment for reflection. "Once the photo comes through what are you doing with it?"

"Circulate it to the RMPs. I'm also thinking about a

search, but where? And is there any point? We don't know if the baby is on the Garrison, if the snatcher is connected to the Army, or lives on the Garrison. We don't even know if the snatcher is male or female. Although female is much more likely."

"He or she might be, though," said Draper thoughtfully, "connected to the Army, that is, so go ahead with that. Talk to Staff Sgt Jones, get a few more patrols on the streets. Show the photo around the Messes, NAFI, that sort of thing."

"Right oh, sir. I'm also going to get Billy to check the CCTV for both incidents, to see if he can find anyone who appears on both of them."

"Good idea, although that may take a while."

"I think it's still worth doing, sir."

"Agreed. I'm willing to throw whatever resources you need at this, Crane. You know and I know how important it is to find Sgt Wainwright's child. So I'm not going to do the 'just get a result' talk bollocks. You know that one, already, eh?"

"Yes, boss."

"Good, now get out of here. You need to be on the ground, not pussyfooting around me."

Crane nodded and did as he was told. As he clattered down the stairs he thought that his Captain was definitely more supportive and less critical than Edwards, but there was a long way to go yet. He just hoped that being an ex NCO, Draper would 'get' the investigative side of the job and support rather than criticise.

After issuing his orders to Jones and Billy, he took himself off to Aldershot Police Station, but managed to call Tina on the way. Just to make sure his wife and son were alright. Were safe at home.

22

BREAKING NEWS
Tonight on BBC South Today.
We are getting reports that a baby has been snatched in North Camp, nr Farnborough. Police say they are investigating and will release full details as soon as they are available. More in our programme at 6.30 tonight.

Bob Wainwright was more than flabbergasted. He was bloody astounded. He felt as though he were in a film, or as though he were watching the events unfolding before him in a drama on the television and hoped that it was happening to someone else. But he knew that it was a vain hope. Because it was real. There really were police officers crawling over his house. There really were a couple of military police lads in a jeep outside on the drive. There really were a clutch of neighbours at the bottom of the street, rubber necking. Trying to find out what was going on. At the other end of the street were the press. Local for now, but apparently the national lot were on their way.

He just hoped that everyone kept out of his garage. They had so far. At least the jeep in front of the garage door might deter them. As he stood on his doorstep, smoking and trying to calm himself, he knew he should be feeling something. His daughter was missing. His daughter could be dead. His daughter could be in the hands of some maniac. But he felt nothing about that. His overriding emotion was fear. Fear focused on the drugs and, of course, on Josip Anic. On what he might do to make sure this deal goes ahead. On how far he would go. On what he might have done already. But he had to push that thought away. Didn't want to believe that Anic could have his daughter. Couldn't voice that thought to anyone.

Taking a last drag of his cigarette, he looked up after he had thrown away the butt and was confronted by the Padre. Shit, fuck, he said in his head, but of his mouth came, "Good afternoon, Padre, thank you for coming, sir," and he held out his hand, hoping the Padre wouldn't notice the tremors.

The two men went into the house and through to where Julie Wainwright was sitting on the settee, leaning on an older woman, the Aldershot Police Family Liaison Officer.

"Julie," Bob said, as he went over to her. "The Padre's here. He's come to see if he can help."

Julie lifted her head off the policewoman's shoulder. Bob had been introduced to her but for the life of him couldn't remember her name. But it didn't seem to matter, he didn't need to speak to her, for she stood and said, "I'll make us all a nice cup of tea," relinquishing her place on the settee to the Padre.

Bob saw the Padre take his wife's hand, watched him rubbing the back of it and then Julie lift her tear stained face to him.

"Why, Padre?" she asked him. "Why would

someone do this?"

"I'm so sorry, Mrs Wainwright. Julie. May I call you Julie?" the Padre asked gently.

Julie nodded, her tears falling off her cheeks and plopping onto her jumper, as she moved her head.

"We must be positive, Julie," he said. "Everyone is working very hard to find out what happened to Tyler."

The Padre had the words of consolation for his wife that Bob was unable to find, let alone voice. Again Julie nodded. It appeared to Bob that she wasn't able to speak. Well neither was he, really. He hoped the Padre wouldn't start asking him questions. Then the phone call came. The one he'd been dreading. From Anic.

"Excuse me, Padre," he said, "I must take this," and he rushed through to the back of the house, pushing past the policewoman in the kitchen, flinging open the door and then answering his mobile.

"Bob!" Julie called after him, but he ignored her wail and kept going until he reached the relatively safety of the garden.

"Yes?" he grunted into the phone.

"Bob, just ringing to see how you are."

"How the hell do you think I am, you bastard."

"Now, now, Bob, that's not the attitude. I've just seen the news and thought I would ring and offer you my condolences."

"For a start my daughter isn't dead so I don't need your bloody condolences and for a second I want to know if you're behind this."

"Me? Bob, how could you think that?"

"Quite easily, I assure you. Now, answer my question. Do you have my daughter?"

"No, Bob, of course not."

"Do you have anything to do with this?"

"Bob, please. What do you take me for?"

Wainwright wanted to spew every expletive he could think of at Anic. But he knew he better not do that. Fear was fuelling his display of bravado. So he kept quiet.

"How is this going to affect our little arrangement?"

Ah, Wainwright thought, this is the real reason he's ringing.

"Could be delayed," he replied. "There are police and military police everywhere. I think we need to lie low for a bit. A few days at least. See what happens here."

"Very well. But don't keep me waiting too long, eh?" Anic said and terminated the call.

Wainwright remained in the garden for a few minutes, smoking and walking around as though the movement would help move the enquiry along, move time along, fast forward to Tyler's return, then Bob could get Anic out of his hair for good

Crying

It had been that easy for Kerry to become whole again. For her to become a mother again. Since her return, the flat seemed to be filled with light, laughter and love. Even Alan had been persuaded to return, no doubt drawn by all the activity and happiness emanating from her and the child, she thought. From Kerry and Tyler.

No one had seemed to notice her as she'd walked back to the flat that afternoon. She seemed invisible as usual. Just another lonely woman walking the streets. Nothing to concern anyone. Her large wrap-around coat had covered Tyler completely and the walking had stopped her crying, so no one was any the wiser about the child she had just taken. Kerry was the one that had understood that all the child had needed was some human contact. Some human contact from her mother. Because that's what Kerry was now. Tyler's mother.

She'd told Alan all about it, when she got home, as she cradled Tyler in her arms. Told him how she'd heard the cry, the one that went straight to her heart. The cry that prompted her into action. The cry that was just for Kerry alone. It must have been, she reasoned, because no one else had reacted to the baby's distress.

No one else had tried to help, she told him. And so it was the cry that had convinced her that this had been her destiny all along. To show she could be a better mother than Julie could ever be. But not only that, it was an opportunity for Alan to be a better father than Bob Wainwright ever wanted to be.

Everything was going to be alright now. Kerry was sure of it.

23

Tonight on Channel 4 News
A baby snatched in broad daylight out of her pushchair.
Did no one see anything? Do we live in a society where no one cares?
A full report later on in the programme.

Billy looked up and stretched as Crane came into the SIB office in Provost Barracks. He yawned, his eyes closing at the height of his deep inhalation of air. Crane looked more closely and saw that Billy looked well and truly knackered.

"You all right, lad?" he asked.

"Mmm, okay thanks, boss."

"Well you don't look it. You look as if you need some fresh air and caffeine. So get a pot of coffee going and we'll take a cup outside."

"Are you sure, boss? I'll keep going."

"Billy, your eyes are practically standing out on stalks. You need a break and I need a coffee. So, the solution is simple. I'll meet you outside and you can tell me what you've found."

Crane was leaning against the Barrack's wall when

Billy emerged with two mugs of steaming coffee in his hand.

"Thanks, Billy."

"Cheers, boss," Billy responded and toasted his mug at Crane.

After blowing on the brew and taking an investigative sip, Crane said, "So, anything for me yet?"

"Yes. Kerry Chandler. The woman we went to talk to about the dead child."

"What about her."

"Well, I've found her on CCTV," Billy said as Crane lit his cigarette. "She was caught up in North Camp in the Co-op. About 10 minutes before Tyler was snatched."

"Shopping?"

"Yes and no, wandering around on her own but I didn't see her buy anything. No kid. No pram."

"Interesting. I wonder where her baby was? She probably got someone to look after her kid for a bit. Molly she's called, isn't she?"

"Yes, boss. But she looked at bit out of it."

"Drugs? Widened pupils? That sort of thing?"

"No, don't think so. The pictures aren't that good, so when I zoom in I can't see her eyes clearly. But she just seems, oh I don't know, lost within herself somehow."

"Well, I guess you get days like that when you've lost your husband."

"True."

"A very interesting co-incidence that, though. Mind you, she does still have a baby. We can't disbelieve our own eyes. We saw what we saw. A baby asleep in the cot."

"That's what I thought. So, I'm going to keep

digging and see what else I can find."

"Thanks, Billy and well done so far."

"No worries, boss. I couldn't live with myself if I missed anything that could have helped find the baby. When I think of my sister's kids and how I'd feel if it was one of them..." Billy's voice trailed off and he examined the bottom of his coffee mug.

"Here, take this would you?" Crane said, to call Billy back from his reverie. He handed back his mug and pulled out his car keys. "I'm off to Aldershot Police Station. We've another press conference. Although I've nothing to tell them. I only hope Anderson has."

Crane was sat at the table, facing the press. Also there were DI Anderson and some bloke from the police press office. He'd briefed them before the event. Told them exactly what to divulge and what not to. As though they were rookies. As though they didn't know how to handle press conferences. Crane had pretty much dismissed his words as soon as they were out of the bloke's mouth. But now? Well he wasn't so sure.

From the minute they'd walked into the room it had started. Cameras whirring and flashing from the photographers bunched up directly in front of the table. Television camera crews were tucked in along the sides of the photographers. Behind them were all the reporters, their mobile phones and hand held recorders pushed towards the police, notebooks open and pencils at the ready.

"DI Anderson!"

"Sgt Major!"

"This way please, sir."

"Could we just have a quote…"

It took some time for the press officer to call them

to order, but in the end had the baying crowd under some sort of control, but only because he'd threatened to cancel the whole thing. When they realised they'd have nothing for their evening news programmes or tomorrow's papers, they settled down, prepared to listen.

But once the prepared statements were out of the way, Crane was shocked by the ferocity of the questions and the tenacity of the reporters laid out before them. Having mostly only had provincial press contact, apart from during Team GB's training camp on the Garrison (which had been a whole other ball game), this was completely different. He was used to Diane Chambers of the Aldershot News nipping at his heels like an angry miniature Yorkshire Terrier. Well, if that's what Chambers was, then this lot were Rottweilers.

They were all represented. Sky, the BBC, ITV, Channel 4 and Channel 5. And not just national reporters but local reporters as well. Crane was well aware that local Aldershot residents would see this press conference twice tonight. Once on the national news programme and again on the local news. See his bumbling display. He hadn't wanted to come over too military, which he thought would have seemed curt and unfeeling to the viewers. But he quickly realised that curt and unfeeling was his normal working mode and when he tried to become softer, more human, it just didn't work. As a result, Anderson and the press officer had fielded most of the many questions and demands and Crane kept his mouth shut for the remainder of the conference.

He wasn't sure if their eager questions were out of concern for the poor parents and for the missing child, or their excitement at such a large news story after a pretty dry news summer. The only other news at the moment was the Party Political Conferences and the television companies probably couldn't believe their luck having such an emotive story to counter balance the dry political news.

The one question they all wanted answering was - when can we interview the parents? They were all desperate to have the sobbing couple degrade themselves on the news programmes. 'It's what our viewers want' they had apparently said to the press officer when making the request. Well, Crane and Anderson were determined to keep the Wainwrights off the television if they could manage it. Plus they didn't want anything upsetting the drugs deal, which still hadn't been completed.

At a nod from the press officer, Crane and Anderson stood and walked out of the room, through a handily located door just to their right, the reporter's questions still following them, until they closed the door and shut them out.

Kerry

Kerry had had to do quite a big shop a couple of days ago. Not wanting to be seen around North Camp for a while, she had gone to the big Asda in Farnborough. It was far more impersonal in there. She'd got lost in the crowds and blended in with all the other harassed shoppers. She had also taken a taxi there and back, to save having to talk to anyone on the bus.

The missing baby seemed to be everyone's topic of conversation and Kerry heard snatches of words. Heard how awful it was. Heard people wondering where Tyler was. Heard mothers telling other mothers that they were too scared to leave their child alone. They wouldn't do it. Not for an instant. Asking how the mother could have done such a thing? Fancy going into a shop and leaving the baby alone outside? Some people linked it to other child snatches. Madeline McCann was on some people's lips. And so the people gossiped away; around the fruit and veg; while squeezing the bread to test it for freshness; while waiting in the queues to pay for their shopping. Kerry had heard similar snippets of conversation when she'd had reason to leave the flat and passed her neighbours on the landing or those congregating around the entrance doors on the ground floor.

But one talked to her. She was still seemingly invisible to most people, her thin waif like appearance making her small and insignificant, perhaps. Ignoring those around her, as they ignored her, Kerry got on with her shopping.

A real live baby had different needs from the two Mollies, Kerry had quickly realised. She'd had to buy more formula (as Tyler had used up what she'd had left over from Molly) and some jars of baby food (Tyler just wasn't satisfied with only a bottle of milk). Luckily she still had the steriliser. And she had to get disposable nappies, of course.

Kerry needed to eat something herself as well. She hadn't really bothered much with food since Molly had died. Not even the arrival of Molly #1 and Molly #2 had managed to ignite an interest in food. But with Tyler around, she was using more energy, so needed food for fuel. A few ready meals kept in the freezer would do the trick.

She'd spent quite a bit of money and when she got home, had managed to get all her bags in the lift with the help of the kind taxi driver. But she'd had to do a few trips back and forth along the landing before all the shopping was safely in the flat.

Alan was worried about the amount of money she must have spent. He'd asked if she really needed to buy so much. But she'd happily told him not to be worried, as she still had quite a lot of the money she'd been given by the Army when he was killed. So there was no reason for him to worry about anything like that at all, it was all taken care of, courtesy of Her Majesty's

Government.

Tyler had grown a lot since Kerry had last seen her with Julie and she was minded to crawl all over the flat and put just about everything she could reach into her mouth. That morning, Kerry had left Molly#1 on the settee, while she went to get her a change of clothes and returned to find Tyler sucking on Molly's toes.

"Look what she's doing," Julie called to Alan and they all had a good laugh at Tyler's antics.

After Kerry had finished changing Molly #1 and put her in the high chair, Tyler pulled herself up by the chair legs and grabbed Molly's feet, clearly wanting to put them in her mouth again. Kerry took her away and put her back on the carpet, but then Tyler thought it was great fun to push Molly #2 around the room in her bouncing chair. It was so nice to see how much Tyler loved the Mollies and wanted to touch them and play with them all the time.

Kerry was tired after the morning's activities (it was much harder looking after three children rather than one baby) and was glad to put Tyler down for her afternoon nap, wanting to spend a bit of time with Alan. Just the two of them. So she put the Mollies in the cot with Tyler, and soon all three of them were fast asleep.

"Come and look at them, Alan," she called and after Alan hobbled his way into the bedroom, they looked down at their three children in the cot. Proud parents at last.

24

This morning on Breakfast. Our reporter Jane Fullerton is in North Camp where a baby was recently snatched in broad daylight. Local residents, police and Army are combing the area in organised searches. We'll be joining Jane at 7.15 am for the latest news.

Julie drifted from room to room, with a pile of clothes in her hand that she should be putting away. But she couldn't remember where they went. Putting them down on her bed, she turned and looked in the mirror at her reflection, but didn't recognise the person looking back at her. The person still dressed in pyjamas, with greasy hair, sunken eyes and chewed lips.

She went down the stairs and took the vacuum out of the cupboard to sweep the carpets, but after looking at it and unable to figure out what she was supposed to do with it, she returned it to its place in the cupboard. She went into the living room and sat on the settee. She turned the television on, then off a few minutes later, unable to concentrate on the inane banal programmes.

She walked back up the stairs and stopped outside Tyler's room. It still had that wonderful baby smell, but the scent was fading fast and with it her hope that her child would be found. Leaning against the door frame she wondered if Tyler missed her mother, as much as her mother missed Tyler.

The weather seemed to be clearing as she looked out of the window. A few lighter clouds were visible as the underlying grey layer broke apart in places. She was desperate to escape the morose feeling that the recent rain had induced in her. It had rattled on the roof for hours without a break. Making her depression worse. Emphasising her aloneness, as she wandered around the house without a purpose. So as the rain had stopped, Julie went back into her bedroom. She pulled on some clothes that were in a pile on the floor and rattled downstairs. She grabbed her raincoat from the hooks near the front door, intending to go out. Immediately the family liaison police officer appeared.

"Julie? Are you alright?"

"Yes thank you," Julie said as firmly as she could, but she was unable to stop the waver in her voice. After clearing her throat she tried again. "I'm fine, I just want a bit of fresh air."

"Oh good, I'll come as well," the woman said. "Just wait while I get my coat."

"Please don't. I want to go out on my own."

"But…"

"I'll be perfectly alright. You better stay here in case there's any news."

Julie grabbed her handbag and ran outside to the car. She wanted to be alone. The police officer was smothering her with her well meaning platitudes and updates from the police every day that never said anything other than, 'the enquiry is progressing'. Progressing where? Progressing how? Basically there was never any news. They were no nearer to finding her baby.

She reached the car. Finding it unlocked she clambered in, threw her handbag on the passenger seat, started the car with the key that was already in the ignition and drove away. Fleeing a house that was so empty since Tyler had been snatched. Bob was never there either. Claiming pressure of work that meant he had to be in his Barracks most of the time. But she knew why he went to work. The real reason. It was because he couldn't face what was happening at home. Couldn't face her. Her depression, loneliness and despair.

She was pretty certain Bob didn't feel the same as she did about the loss of Tyler. It didn't seem to have made much of an impression on his emotions. But then nothing did anymore. Since Tyler was born, he'd retreated into himself. Instead of putting his new born child first, he'd put himself first, thereby making sure Tyler had very little impact on his life.

Julie decided to go to the woodland at the top of Farnborough, hoping for sunshine and bird song to soothe her battered psyche. She'd known no peace since Tyler had been snatched. She not only blamed herself, but she knew Bob blamed her as well. In fact Padre Symmonds was the only person who hadn't blamed her. He'd tried to tell her that it wasn't her fault. Wasn't because of anything she'd done or not done. Told her that the blame lay with the person who had snatched Tyler. But she didn't believe him. After all she was the one who had left Tyler outside the shop, while she was buying pasties of all things! She'd never eaten that pasty. In fact she didn't think she'd ever be able to eat a pasty again.

She left the Garrison and was driving up the dual carriageway towards Tesco when the rain started again, the deluge making her realise she was in trouble. Realise that she had badly misjudged the weather. Once again the ferocity of the rain was relentless, falling from a sky filled with angry clouds that were so low she felt she could touch them.

She slowed down as the road rapidly filled with water, the drains unable to cope with the sudden return of the storm. Driving became impossible as great rivers of water lay in wait to catch out unwitting motorists. The wipers, frantic in their attempt to push the rain from the windscreen, did nothing to help clear the rain streaked view of the road, which was faint and wavering in the eerie half light. Cars tiptoed past on the other side of the dual carriageway, their pale faced drivers just visible as they hunched over the steering wheel.

Unable to see where she was going, Julie stopped the car in the middle of the road. It wasn't even possible to pull into the kerb which was awash with water. The rain threw itself at her car and as the storm intensified so did the noise. Her car and her head were filled with it and she became trapped in its clutches. Trapped inside the car with her thoughts. Thoughts of her baby, her husband and illegal drugs. She screamed and screamed and screamed in a vain effort to make them go away.

Kim had also badly misjudged the weather, thinking she could quickly walk into Aldershot during a break in the rain. She was waiting to cross the dual carriageway at the pedestrian crossing hoping the lights would turn red and stop the traffic, when the rain came down. She quickly put up her umbrella, but the rain was so hard, it was barely any use. She looked down to see the water on the road rising and threatening to over flow onto the pavement. Her trainers and jeans were of little use against the rain and both were already sopping wet. As she lifted her head to see if she could walk across the road yet, a car stopped by the crossing. Which was strange as the traffic lights were still green. Looking more closely Kim realised the driver was Julie Wainwright and that she was screaming uncontrollably.

Kim reacted without thinking. She pulled open the driver's door and squatted down so her face was level with Julie's, keeping her umbrella up to try and shield them both from the rain.

"Julie," she shouted. But when that got no reaction, she shook Julie's shoulder, which seemed to do the trick. Julie stopped screaming and looked blankly at her.

"Julie," she shouted over the rain. "I'm Kim Symmonds, the Padre's wife. Here scoot over into the passenger seat and I'll take you home."

Pushing Julie into complying, Kim clambered into the car. Her wet jeans clung to her legs and her trainers squelched as she pressed the pedals.

Kim covered the short distance to the Wainwright's house in a few minutes, frantic to get Julie home out of the cascading rain. Kim glanced to her left, to see Julie shivering uncontrollably and moaning softly. Her dark hair was dyed blacker by the rain and the water dripping from it mingled with her tears. The poor woman was in such distress, Kim considered taking her straight to hospital, but feared it would take too long to get to Frimley Park Hospital. Home was best. Once there she could get Julie dry and into a warm bed and then call out a doctor. Pulling up onto the Wainwright's drive, she ran around the car and pulled open the passenger door, helping Julie out. Together they stumbled to the front door, which was thrown open by the policewoman.

"Oh, thank God, you've found her," she said. "I put out a call to the patrol cars when the storm started in the hope they'd find her and bring her home."

They bundled Julie up the stairs, where they stripped off her soaking clothes and wrapped her in a towelling bathrobe before putting her to bed. Julie was still shaking and moaning as the policewoman left the room to call an ambulance.

"It's all my fault," Julie whispered to Kim, grabbing at her arm. "All my fault. I should never have left her alone. Where's my baby? Why can't anyone find my baby?" Kim had no answer for her, so did the best she could, stroking Julie's still damp hair and making soothing noises while she waited for help to arrive.

Self Esteem

Kerry wished Alan was a bit more help around the house and with the children. To be honest she was getting a bit pissed off with him just sitting in his chair all day. She'd also like a bit more time to herself. Being a mother was fulfilling, of course it was and never let anyone say that she was a bad mother, but today she was really exhausted and could do with some help.

She'd just completed the morning routine, getting the two Mollies up and about, changing and feeding Tyler and she was sitting limply on the settee, surfing the television channels to find something to watch.

She knew she looked rough today. Had seen Alan's look. The one he used to give her when he was alive. The 'I think you could make a bit more of your appearance' look. He had a look for everything. There was the 'oh, so you haven't done the housework yet' look and the 'shouldn't you have made the beds by now' look.

She tried to smooth down her completely untameable red hair. She knew she should go to the hairdressers, but she just never seemed to have the time, or the energy. She seemed to be on the go 24/7.

Picking up her mug of coffee she saw her nails were broken and some of them were cracked. Putting the coffee back down on the floor, she rubbed her hands together and just as she suspected, the sides of her fingers were rough to the touch, all dry and split and the skin on the backs of her hands was sore.

She looked down at her dress which had white bleach spots on it and the slippers on her feet were falling to pieces. No wonder Alan was signalling his disapproval. She was a complete wreck. Well, if he wanted her to do something with herself, he'd just have to pull his weight.

Looking over, she saw he was sat there in his chair. Molly #2 was in the highchair and Molly #1 the bouncing chair. She thought she'd give them a change of scenery this morning and had swapped them over. Tyler was sitting in the playpen surrounded by some toys and was happily chewing on a teething ring.

Here was her opportunity, she decided. If he wanted her to do something with herself, he'd just have to help. She jumped off the settee and went over to him, climbing on his knee and kissing his face. She had to be careful where she kissed him and took care to avoid the bits of cheek that had been flayed off by the IED.

"I was just wondering, Alan, if you could do me a favour?" she asked, squirming around to get comfortable. One of his thigh bones was poking through the skin and had pierced his trousers, so she put her weight on the other leg so as not to hurt him or herself.

He seemed happy with her attention, so she continued, "I really need to go the hairdresser's Alan. I just can't manage my hair anymore. It's all over the place. So," she said coyly, "I was wondering if you'd mind the children for me. Just for an hour. I could pop up to the local salon. I'm sure they'll fit me in. After all I want to look my best for you."

Alan smiled by way of reply, so she took that as a yes, grabbed her coat and bag and skipped out of the apartment before he could change his mind.

The salon was empty when Kerry arrived and the staff fell on her eagerly when she said she wanted a wash, cut and blow dry. They even persuaded her to have her nails sorted out. Kerry drew the line at false nails, so the manicurist said she would make them all the same length, buff them and put a light polish on.

Kerry felt like a model, as one woman attended to her hair and another her nails, both at the same time.

"So, do you live around here?" the hairdresser asked, whose name was Jude, according to her name badge.

"Yes, just down the road," Kerry replied.

"Oh, right, it's just that I've not seen you in here before." Jude looked at Kerry in the mirror.

"No," said Kerry.

"Bit busy, I suppose?" asked Jude, her head going from side to side as she inspected Kerry's hair.

"Mmm." replied Kerry watching the manicurist.

"Kids?"

"Mmm." Kerry turned her attention back to the hairdresser and was concerned that maybe Jude was cutting too much hair off. There seemed to be a lot of it on the floor.

"Hubby looking after them, then?"

"What?" Kerry turned her attention back to Jude. "Oh, yes," she agreed.

"Shame about that kid. Have you heard?"

"What kid?" The manicurist had now started on

Kerry's other hand, so Kerry was inspecting the one she'd finished.

"You know, the one that's gone missing."

"Mmm." Kerry wondered if her nails were too short as well as her hair.

"Terrible, that. What do you think?"

"I think you need to be careful with my hair. I don't want it too short," Kerry rebuked her.

"Sorry, I'm sure," replied Jude sniffing but she dutifully turned her attention back to her scissors.

Kerry left the hairdressers and had to admit they'd done a good job. She could see her hair in the shop windows, the shining curls bouncing up and down, finishing just above her shoulders. It should be more manageable, she thought, if I put some of that anti frizz stuff I've seen advertised on the telly on it. So she decided to treat herself to some. She wandered around the local Boots store. It was only small, but seemed to stock quite a large hair product range and it took Kerry a while to choose which product to buy.

While she was waiting to pay she looked down to admire her nails, and that's when she caught sight of her dress. She still had the one on that was covered in bleach spots. She wondered if the local charity shop had anything nice in, so as she wandered out of Boots, she decided to turn right. There were two charity shops in that street, she was sure she'd find something there.

She was right. Not only did she find a couple of dresses for herself, but some lovely baby clothes for the girls. The lady volunteer in the shop said they'd just been handed in that morning and wasn't she lucky to get them.

Glancing at her watch as she left the second charity shop, Kerry realised she'd been much longer than she'd intended to be, over two hours already, so she better hurry back to Alan and the girls.

Accident

The flat was very quiet when Kerry got back. She thought Alan must have been doing a great job to get all three babies so happy and contented.

"Well, what do you think?" she asked Alan as she twirled in front of him. She patted her hands under her hair and then flapped them in his face.

"I even got my nails done," she trilled. "I hope you like them."

Alan didn't reply. Undaunted, Kerry showed him her purchases. Firstly the hair products and then secondly the baby clothes.

"I thought this would look particularly good on Tyler," she said, holding up a white frilly dress with matching knickers to go over her nappy. "Let me just hold it to her and make sure it fits. Is she awake?"

Kerry turned to the play pen, expecting to see the child sitting there, playing with her toys, just as she left her. But Tyler was lying on her back. Motionless.

"Oh, of course, silly me, she's fallen asleep."

As she leaned over the cot she saw a large dark stain on the mattress, by Tyler's head.

"Oh dear, has she been sick, Alan? Perhaps she

threw up her milk from this morning?"

She turned back to Alan, who still hadn't spoken. As she looked more closely at his face she saw a single tear rolling down his cheek.

"Alan?" she asked in alarm. "Alan? What's happened?"

When he still didn't reply, she turned back to the baby. As she picked Tyler up, her head flopped backwards, just like a new born and Kerry had to support it. There was something sticky on the back of her head.

"Alan?" she asked again. Clutching the child to her she looked more closely at the dark stain, realising it might be blood.

"What's that? Is it blood? What happened?"

A tear rolled down Alan's other cheek this time, as he haltingly told her what had happened.

"Tyler had been standing up holding the rail," he said. "I watched her try to take a couple of steps but then she tottered unsteadily, and fell backwards onto the bar."

"The bar?" whispered Kerry.

"Yes," Alan said. "The bit that has hinges that click into place, the part that should have had a piece of padded fabric on."

Kerry went pale as she realised she had forgotten to popper it in place.

"I'm so sorry," he said. "I tried to get up, but just couldn't. No matter how hard I tried, I was stuck here. Stuck in this chair. My legs just didn't seem to work today. I think it was walking on them when we got Tyler. I must have done even more damage to them, as I've not been able to use them since."

"Never mind, Alan," she consoled him, realising that

she was partly to blame. "I guess Tyler was always meant to be like the Mollies. Reborn. And anyway, if the truth be told, I was getting a bit tired of looking after three kids under one year old. I'm not sure I was coping very well, was I Alan?"

"You did your best," he said, which made Kerry's heart swell and tears prick her own eyes.

"Thanks, Alan. No one can say I didn't try. I gave it my best shot. Don't worry, it's not your fault."

She picked a clean blanket off the dryer, wrapped Tyler in it and put her back into the playpen.

"Come on, Alan, cheer up and look on eBay with me. We'll find a replacement for her. I'll bring the laptop over to you."

As she turned on the computer she mused, "I'm not sure I can leave Tyler on the Garrison church steps, like I did Molly. I'll have to think of somewhere else to put her."

25

Today on Good Morning Britain.
The village of North Camp and surrounding areas have been transformed from a quiet backwater. People are coming in their hundreds from the neighbouring towns of Farnborough and Aldershot to help in the organised searches for baby Tyler. A source close to the police has said that there is little hope of finding her alive if she's been abandoned outdoors. However everyone coming to help search day after day continues to be upbeat and hopeful of a happy ending.

"No news yet," seemed to be Crane's mantra, when speaking to people about the stolen, kidnapped, or snatched baby. It didn't much matter what you called the appalling crime, the reply was the same. No news yet. Crane was at the stage of dragging himself into work every day. And it wasn't just the fact he'd usually only grabbed about four hours of sleep. He felt like he was wading through everyone's guilt as he walked across the office. Guilt because they hadn't found Tyler yet. Guilt because, as everyone knew, the longer it took to find the child, the more than likely they were to find a dead body than a living baby. So moral went down, as the days ticked by, hour by hour by hour.

There had been a summing up piece on the breakfast television channels that morning about the case. He'd watched it with Tina. The presenters had detailed what had been done to try and find Tyler so far: exhaustive searches in the local area by police, military and civilian volunteers; appeals to the public for anyone who may have seen Tyler being snatched or someone running away from the scene with or without a baby; posters with Tyler's photograph on plastered all around the immediate area and beyond, particularly around large superstores; interviewing of local registered nonce's; all the appeals that had been made on the local and national television, radio and in the newspapers. And still nothing.

Tina watched, white faced, next to him at the table and at the end of the piece turned to him. But no words came out of her mouth. No questions. No reprisals. And for that he was grateful. He smiled his thanks, stood, kissed her and Daniel goodbye and left for work.

That morning Captain Draper joined them downstairs and so all three of them, Draper, Crane and Billy sat disconsolately around the crowded white boards that Crane so loved, yet now hated, as they mocked him and his inability to find the child.

"So, nothing? No news? No leads?"

Draper seemed to want it confirmed, so Crane did the honours. "No, sir, nothing."

"Let's try and look at things another way, then. Is there anything we haven't done that we could have done?" Draper stood and walked over to the boards. "If we still think there could be a connection between the dead baby and the snatched baby, how about those lists you were working on. The ones of any soldiers who had had a baby recently."

"They all checked out, sir," Billy said. "The only thing we can say about those enquiries is that one of the mothers, um," Billy consulted his notes, "Kerry Chandler, was also seen in the Co-op in North Camp about 10 minutes before Tyler was snatched."

"But no other sighting of her on CCTV after that?"

"No, sir, but she could have been shielded by other shoppers or vehicles. Sorry, sir."

"I think we should visit her again," said Crane, absently worrying at his scar.

"Why? She checked out the first time around. You even saw her baby," Draper said.

"I know, but there's just something about her," Crane replied.

"Apart from the fact that she acts like a mad woman, you mean?" said Billy.

Crane smiled for the first time that day. "What do you think, boss?" he asked Draper.

"I think we should see if we have enough to get a search warrant."

"Why?" Crane frowned. "I'm talking about more of an informal door to door. We can even take some locals with us, if you like. Get them to talk to the other residents in the block as well."

"Because a visit could spook her, informal or formal, if she really does have Tyler. I won't authorise anything that could potentially put the child in jeopardy."

"But we're not going to get a search warrant on Billy's assessment that she looks like a mad woman and because she was seen in North Camp shopping that morning. Along with a few hundred other people. I just thought Billy and I could go, as we've already met her. We could have a friendly chat and a surreptitious look around. Come on, boss."

Crane waited as Draper tapped his foot and then drummed his fingers on top of one of the white boards. At last he seemed to come to a decision.

"No can do. See DI Anderson. Find out if he can get a search warrant."

Draper's clipped instructions felt like a slap in the face and Crane had to deliberately harden his features into a mask of respect as he said, "Very well, sir."

Anderson wasn't any more helpful when Crane rang him to ask about getting a search warrant for Kerry Chandler's flat. "I'll look into it, but from memory, I doubt that we have enough to go on for authorisation for the search."

"How long will it take to get one, if we do have enough?" Crane growled.

Fed up with what appeared to be a second 'no' response to his idea. He'd thought at least Anderson would be on his side.

"A few days, to be honest. Come on, Crane, no one is going to be willing to authorise a search warrant for something that could potentially set an unstable widow off. If she does have Tyler, God knows what she might do if she were cornered."

"Alright, alright, don't labour the point. Anyway if we're throwing bricks about, what about your surveillance of Anic. Anything there that could lead us to believe he took the Wainwright's kid?"

"Not a bloody thing. If anything he's become whiter than white. He's only going between the offices of his import/export business, the car repair shop and home. Even his enforcers seem to be having a holiday from violence. No scraps, damage to premises, threats to take over any other businesses. Sweet FA as they say."

"Alright, thanks, Derek. I'll be in touch," and Crane ended the very unsatisfactory call. He decided to sleep on it overnight, but knew that he would more than likely go with Billy to see Kerry Chandler. Sod authorisation. He needed to find that child and she was the only, albeit miniscule, lead they had.

26

WHERE IS BABY TYLER?
By our Chief Investigative Reporter Diane Chambers
Here at the Aldershot News, we would like to publically thank everyone who is coming day after day to help in the search for baby Tyler. We now understand that the focus of the search has changed from outdoor and wooded areas to the many local houses and flats. Police and Army personnel are going from door to door in the hope of finding neighbours who might have seen a baby suddenly arrive in a house near them.
So we urge local residents to question what is happening in your area. Can you help find baby Tyler? Has a baby suddenly appeared in your area? Does she look anything like Tyler? If you can help please call Aldershot Police.

Kim watched as Francis stuffed the last of his gear into his kit bag, laying his bible on the top before pulling it closed. "Right," he said. "I think that's everything."

This was the first time he was going away on exercise since they'd married. He would be gone for a week. Kim had asked where he was going and why, but only got generalities in reply, not specifics. That was an interesting role reversal for her. Having previously been the one to say to her family that she was off on exercise, but hoped they understood she couldn't say where or why. It definitely put a whole new spin on life and she smiled wryly to herself as she followed Francis down the stairs, now understanding how it must have made her parents feel. Left out. Shut out of a part of their daughter's life.

Francis dumped his kit by the front door and they went into the kitchen to have a final cup of coffee together. Kim feeling unusually emotional. For once instead of going away herself, she was now the one being left behind, left alone, which was a whole new ball game, as the saying goes.

"Right," he said after taking a slurp of his coffee. "I've cleared my diary, so there should be no worries there. You can make appointments for me from, say, oh, best make it the beginning of the month. Okay?"

"Yes, boss," she said grinning and pulling at an imaginary forelock, which brought a smile to his unusually serious looking face. "No worries, boss. After all I was an office manager for a whole team of men, so I'm sure I can handle one officer. Although, it should be said, a very important officer." She tried to keep her face serious, but ended up bursting out laughing at the look of horror on his face. "Oh, Francis," she said, "I was only teasing."

He managed a quick smile, but then said, "Kim, um, will you be alright? I know it's the first time I've been away since we got married, but you knew all about this life when you married me…didn't you?"

Kim heard the pleading in his voice and watched him fiddle with the wedding ring on her finger as her hand lay in his and knew it was her job to reassure him.

"Of course, Francis, don't be silly," she put on her

best ex-sergeant's voice. "I'll be perfectly alright, sir. I am perfectly capable, you know."

"Yes I do, darling, I do," he said as he smiled and then stood to leave.

"Oh, one last thing before you go," she said.

"Mmm?" He seemed distracted as he went out into the hall.

"I'd like to see Julie Wainwright, see if I can offer some support. Just while you're not here," she said quickly. "I wouldn't want to butt in."

"What?" his back was turned to her and he was picking up his kitbag. "Of course you're not butting in," he said straightening and turning to her. "Thanks for offering, it means a lot. I'm very worried about her."

"I know you are, I'll support her the best I can until you come back."

He kissed her goodbye quickly, walked out of the door and down the path, his kit slung over his back. Once, twice, he glanced over his shoulder at her and the life he was leaving behind. Kim could see there was sadness in his eyes at the leaving, but also excitement in the going. In those few steps between wife and car he went from belonging to Kim back to belonging to the Army. She squinted in the sun and waved him goodbye until she couldn't see the car any longer. As she stood there the sun went behind a cloud, making her shiver, so she went back into the house and closed the door behind her.

Now it was Kim's turn to be strong for others and to be there for those Francis was not around to help. Others such as Julie Wainwright, who she knew Francis had been particularly upset about leaving. She would take strength from the knowledge that he would be with her in spirit, the entire time he was away, in everything that she did.

Sitting with Julie Wainwright was like sitting with someone who was not 25 years old, but more like 55. Her eyes were distant, her face had fallen in on itself, her hair was plastered to her head and her hands shook slightly as she reached out for her mug of tea. Having a conversation with her meant trying to fill in the blanks.

"Do you think..?" she asked but didn't finish the sentence. Then she said, "Have they found..?" Finally she managed, "Is there any news?"

Kim had to shake her head. "No, not yet, Julie. But look, I worked with the Branch for a long time and I know that Sgt Major Crane and Billy, in fact all of the team, are doing their very best to find Tyler as quickly as they can. They've made all sorts of enquiries and all sorts of appeals. They're keeping her name and picture in the papers day after day and there are teams of squaddies searching everywhere they can think of. The whole Garrison has been mobilised to help find Tyler."

"I know. Everyone is being very kind. I just hope..." And Julie's eyes became distant again and her body slumped as she curled up, mumbling words Kim could only faintly hear and anyway didn't make any sense. The family liaison police officer had told Kim the doctor had given Julie strong tranquilisers, as it was the only way to calm her down. It wasn't very nice to see her like this, she'd confided, but it was better than the wild, distraught woman she'd been before.

Kim sat next to Julie, holding her hand, rubbing it absently, looking through the window at the rapidly changing weather. When she'd left home storm clouds had been building and the wind had been getting up, blowing the autumn leaves from the trees. As they sat on the settee the light began to fade outside and it started to rain. Or so Kim thought. But the rattle on the glass was much louder than from rain. She stood and walked to the window, astonished to see that hailstones were battering the glass. As she watched them pile up on the pavement and the road, they turned the world white as though it was covered by deep mid-winter snow. But instead of the muffled sounds and feelings brought on by a blanket of snow, the hailstones bounced and crashed onto the roofs of nearby houses. They smashed into cars, striking the metal with a hollow ring. They flew through the trees and bounced off the road and pathways. The street was eerily empty, as no one seemed willing to risk the stinging pain of the hailstones.

As Kim watched and marvelled at the bizarreness of the weather, it was hard not to mull over the weird synchronicity of Tyler being snatched, just as Kim had been, during her last and what turned out to be her final investigation with the Branch. Kim had been left to rot in the middle of nowhere, hoping that she would be found. Clinging to the hope that Crane and the Padre would find her in time. She just hoped Tyler hadn't been left to rot somewhere outside and without shelter. If she had, she'd surely be dead by now from cold and dehydration. Try as she might Kim couldn't shake the picture in her head of tiny Tyler rotting away somewhere in a shallow grave that by now would be covered with a blanket of white, ice cold, hailstones.

27

Later on BBC News – Missing Baby Tyler – new hope as telephone calls from local residents flood into the Aldershot Police Station. They are responding to an appeal for neighbours to question any sudden appearance of a baby in their neighbourhood and urging them to report anything suspicious to the police.

"You're sure about this, boss?" Billy asked as they walked along the landing to Kerry's flat.

"Never been surer, Billy," Crane said. "If nothing else, I've got to rid myself of the feeling that Kerry has something to do with all this - the baby left at the church and the disappearance of Tyler. And I won't rest until I see with my own eyes what's going on in that flat."

"Okay, boss."

"So, remember, this is just a friendly visit. We're calling just to see how she is, nothing formal about it."

"Boss," acknowledged Billy although Crane could see the doubt in his eyes. Everyone in the office knew that Draper and Anderson had forbidden any further contact with Kerry. As far as the two men were concerned there was insufficient evidence for a search warrant, or for interviewing her. But Crane disagreed. The fact that Kerry had been seen on CCTV on the Garrison the morning the baby had been left at the church and in the Co-op in North Camp 10 minutes before Tyler had been snatched was too much of a coincidence for Crane. So he and Billy were out on a limb here. Following up Crane's hunch.

Crane stopped at Kerry's door and rang the doorbell. "Remember, Billy," he hissed. "Nice and friendly does it. Be your most charming - that's an order."

As a result he and Billy were both smiling naturally when Kerry answered the door.

"Morning, Kerry," Crane said. "Hope you don't mind, but Sgt Williams and I were in the area and thought we'd just catch up with you. See how you're doing. How's everything? Can we come in?" and before Kerry had time to argue Crane had manoeuvred the three of them into her small living room.

"Oh, right, yes, thanks," Kerry mumbled. "Um, do you want tea?"

"That would be nice, thanks," Crane said looking around the room while Kerry was busy in the kitchen. The room wasn't as chaotic as before, but still looked a mess, as though someone had made an attempt at tidying up, but never finished the job. There were piles of magazines and newspapers in one corner of the room. Opened and unopened post lay under the coffee table. Muslin cloths were draped over the settee, which was now covered with a garish throw, presumably to hide the rips in the fabric, Crane surmised. Opposite the settee and next to the one armchair in the room was a highchair with a baby in it.

Crane studied it for some moments from his place

near the door. The child was dressed in a pink all in one suit. In front of the child was a small plastic bowl with mashed food in and a pink plastic spoon by its side. The child seemed unusually still. She, for Crane assumed it was Kerry's baby girl Molly, was looking straight ahead, but Crane didn't see her blink. Maybe she had when he'd looked around the room. Or shared a knowing look with Billy. Or watched Kerry and her bouncing ringlet curls as she went to make the tea. Try as he might to spot it, though, he couldn't catch the child blinking.

Molly's arms were outstretched with one of them resting on the plastic tray of the high chair. A curled fist next to the pink spoon. Again Crane watched for a movement of the hand, an uncurling of the fingers, or a grab for the spoon. But saw nothing. The hand didn't budge. Just as the eyes didn't blink.

As Kerry came back from the kitchen with two mugs in her hand, Crane opened his mouth to ask about the baby when Billy said, "Thanks for the drink, Kerry. Um, is everything alright?"

"Yes, of course," she replied, looking at him askance. "Why?"

"It's just that when we came in I got a whiff of smoke."

"Oh, that," Kerry laughed, the strange hollow tone of it, making her sound slightly maniacal. "I burned the toast this morning and I've been trying to get rid of the smell ever since."

"I see," Billy said, but Crane could see Billy wasn't convinced.

"How's Molly?" Crane asked.

"Oh, lovely as ever, thank you," Kerry replied, a smile breaking over her face. In that smile Crane could see what he saw in his wife Tina's smile. Love and pride for her child.

"Good, but it's just that…" and for once Crane faltered. He was finding social small talk with a possible suspect difficult.

"Just what?"

"She seems very still."

"How can you tell?" Kerry looked very perplexed.

"Pardon?" Crane was unsure where this bizarre conversation was going.

"She's in the bedroom, so how can you tell she's very still?"

"No, she's in the high chair."

Crane was beginning to have a real sense of the woman's madness. He was standing a foot away from a highchair with Molly in it. A Molly that wasn't blinking, moving or making a sound. The child's hair was exactly the same as in her photograph near the television. Molly's cheeks had a lovely bloom to them and she was just perfect in every sense. Apart from the fact she was as still as a statue. Crane just couldn't understand it.

"Oh, I see now," Kerry said.

Crane didn't see at all, so kept quiet, waiting for an explanation.

"That's a doll in the high chair. It's not Molly," and Kerry smiled. An impish grin, as though she was pleased to have outwitted Crane.

"Bloody hell," Crane's surprise was genuine and he took the two strides to the high chair. He stretched out a hand tentatively and stroked Molly's face. His finger, instead of warm, pliant flesh, met with cold hard plastic and he involuntarily jumped back.

Grinning, Billy joined him and took hold of the doll's arm, waving it up and down. "Hello Sgt Major

Crane," Billy said in his best Punch and Judy voice, making Kerry laugh.

"It's so life like," he said to Kerry.

"I know, it's really good, isn't it. They're called reborn dolls," she replied.

"Never heard of them."

"Neither had I," said Kerry. "I found them on the internet."

It was Billy who brought back some reality to the conversation. "So where's Molly?" he asked.

"Why, she's asleep in her cot," Kerry said, indicating the bedroom.

Before she could object, Billy opened the bedroom door, quickly followed by Crane and they both bundled into the cramped room. Lying in a cot was a larger baby, at least from the outline of the body. The signature blond curls were spread across the top of the mattress. Crane indicated with his head for Billy to stand in the doorway, blocking Kerry's access to the room. He then reached out and put a hand on the blanket covering the child. To his relief and if he was honest, astonishment, the blanket moved up and down under his hand. The child was breathing. Leaning over the cot to better see Molly's face, she had a healthy glow about her and beautiful eye lashes on her closed eyes. Crane stood still for a moment, but she kept breathing, so he had no choice but to back out of the room.

"Sorry," he said, closing the bedroom door. "It's alright right, I didn't wake her up."

"Good," said Kerry, "it took me a while to get her to sleep."

"I'll take the mugs back," Billy said, grabbing their drinks and walking into the kitchen, while Crane engaged Kerry in baby talk. After a couple of minutes, he returned and said, "Well, we better be on our way, boss. Leave Kerry here to her chores."

"Right, oh," Crane said. Turning to Kerry he continued, "Thanks for the tea and for the fright over the doll," he grinned. "Take care and if we can help at all, give us a shout. After all Alan was one of ours and we'll do what we can for you."

Kerry nodded, her eyes filling with tears, as she shut the door on them.

Crane and Billy didn't speak until they turned the corner on the landing. When they did they both spoke at once.

"Bloody hell," said Billy.

"Jesus Christ," said Crane.

Crane shook his head. "I could have sworn that doll was real. I've never seen anything like it. I'll have to look up those reborn dolls on the internet."

"Damn creepy if you ask me, boss. Anyway there was nothing in the kitchen, nor in the bathroom. No Tyler and nothing to suggest that Tyler had ever been there."

"Nothing unusual at all?"

"No. Just a normal kitchen with fridge and cooker in. What seemed to be a chest freezer was pushed in that utility bit the flats have, just off the kitchen. The whole place is just in a muddle, really. Stuff plonked anywhere. The bathroom was full of toiletries and towels, but again, nothing out of the ordinary. And definitely no snatched child."

"Oh well, at least we had a look. What was that smell, by the way. I didn't smell anything."

"I don't know. It was just a lingering odour really, but I don't think it smelled of burnt toast."

"What did it smell of, then?"

"You're not going to believe me, boss."

"Go on, give me a try."

"Burnt flesh."

"You're right, Billy. I don't believe you. Don't you start going mad on me as well."

They reached the car and Crane drove back to Provost Barracks, deep in thought. He'd tried and found nothing. But he still had this disquieting feeling that all was not right in Kerry's world. Crane couldn't get over how real that reborn doll looked. And how much she looked like the dead child from the church. But he had no explanation for a breathing baby in the cot. It must be Molly. Mustn't it?

28

The only thing they had, as far as Crane was concerned, was his disquiet over Kerry Chandler. But he was the only one. No one else agreed with him.

He'd received the expected dressing down from Dan Draper for going to Kerry's flat with Billy. Without authorisation. Against orders. The Captain hadn't fallen back on his NCO days with any of the understanding Crane had hoped for. He'd well and truly become an officer. Crane was still stinging from the heated exchanges. Previously Draper had taken to calling Crane, Tom, which had moved their relationship to an even friendlier basis. Or so Crane had thought. That security of an understanding relationship with his new Captain had been shattered as soon as Crane stepped out of line.

Despite the telling off, Crane had continued his investigation. He'd spent a snatched couple of hours on the internet at home, learning all he could about reborn dolls. He'd found that many reborn owners were simply doll collectors, while others had gone through miscarriages, had no means for adoption, or suffered from empty nest syndrome. The dolls became substitute children, forever babies who would never grow. To Crane's surprise some women dressed the dolls, washed their hair and even took them for walks in pushchairs.

Reborn hobbyists, as they were called, named the emotional response to holding their dolls 'cuddle therapy'. It seemed studies suggested cuddling a baby caused a release of hormones which produced a sense of emotional well being and some psychologists believed that this could happen with realistic dolls as well. One psychiatrist explained that mothering a real newborn baby released the hormone oxytocin in the mother and hypothesized that this may explain why 'reborn mothers' become emotionally attached to their reborn dolls.

Of particular relevance to Kerry was the opinion that grieving parents could form emotional bonds with reborn dolls, substituting their deceased child with the doll. Some grief counsellors used them to symbolise a step in the grieving process. However, if a woman who had lost a baby grew too attached to their reborn, it could indicate their grief was not getting resolved. In that case, the likeness of the doll to the deceased child risked being harmful by becoming a permanent replacement for the grieving parents.

Crane didn't feel quite so stupid when he read that reborn dolls looked so real they had been mistaken for real babies. In July 2008, police in Australia smashed a car window to rescue what seemed like an unconscious baby only to find it was a reborn doll. The police stated that the doll was 'incredibly lifelike' and that bystanders who thought a baby was dying were frightened by the incident. A similar episode was reported in the United States in which police broke the window of a Hummer to save a baby that turned out to be a reborn doll.

Some psychiatrists stated it was typical to think something is weird or creepy when it's unknown, far from the norm, or common only to a different culture. It was natural for people to find ways of preserving memories of those they loved - from making photo albums, to visiting gravesites, to keeping an urn of ashes on the mantel.

But, Crane wondered, could an inanimate doll - one so realistic as to look alive - really replace a living being? In many ways, such a thought reminded him of a scene from the films Stepford Wives or Invasion of the Body Snatchers. It was a disturbing thought to have something that was not alive, take the place of a real human.

He decided to talk to Tina about it, so that night he gave her the information he'd printed out. She sat in the kitchen and read through it while he tidied up.

"Tom, this is really giving me the creeps. Are you seriously thinking that Kerry has replaced her dead child with a reborn doll?"

"I'm afraid I am. The question is how do I go forward on this one? I wanted to talk to the Padre about it, but he's still away on exercise at the moment. I'm not sure what Draper will make of it, so I might run it past Derek first."

"Will that theory give you any basis for making a case against Kerry for manslaughter of her daughter Molly? And don't forget you saw Molly in her cot."

"Did I though, Tina? Perhaps that was a reborn doll as well."

"At least you didn't find Tyler there."

"No, but I wish I had. I've absolutely no idea where she is or who may have her. Kerry was my one lead on that case as well. But there was no sign of Tyler anywhere in the flat."

"It seems there's no sign of Tyler in any flat or house in the local area," Tina beckoned to the copy of the Daily Mail on the kitchen table, where the disappearance of Tyler Wainwright was still front page news.

"Have you any idea how many calls are coming in from articles like that? The paper asking everyone to question what is happening in their neighbourhood. Bloody Diane Chambers has started something yet again."

"Hasn't it helped?"

"Helped? Every bloody nutter in the area is calling about children playing outside their door, babies crying at night and pregnant mothers who've just come back from the hospital after giving birth! The trouble is they're tying up valuable resources. We've had to have extra telephone lines channelled into the police station and Anderson has had to enlist extra bodies from other local stations. And they are already stretched to the limit as it is what with the searches and door knocking. We might get a lead from the appeal," he ran his hands through his hair. "But what if that lead is buried under an avalanche of useless information?" He began pacing the kitchen. "How long do you think it will take us to find that one lead that is actually useful under all this dross?" Crane's voice became louder as his frustration took over and he reached out and swept the offending paper off the table.

Derek was rather more pragmatic about Crane's theories, when he talked to him about the reborn doll Crane had seen in Kerry's flat.

"Sorry, Crane, I just can't see it."

"See what exactly, Derek?"

"See that Kerry has replaced Molly with a re-born doll. I can't get around the fact you and Billy saw a larger baby in the cot and when you touched it, you could feel the baby breathing. Until you can explain that to me, there's nothing for us to go on."

"There's only one thing that would confirm if Kerry is the mother of the dead child found at the church and that's DNA."

"I know that, Crane, but you haven't got a basis for getting any sort of warrant. You can't just go around taking people's DNA on a hunch."

"What if I can get it another way?"

"What other way?"

"I don't know yet, I'll think on it."

29

This morning on Breakfast.
How are the parent's of baby Tyler coping? They haven't been seen in public since their daughter's disappearance. Later in the programme friends and relatives talk to us about how Julie and Bob Wainwright are faring.

There was no getting away from it. It was time for Tyler's parents to do an appeal on television for the safe return of their child. Despite extensive appeals by the police and media, nothing had been found to give them any sort of lead as to Tyler's whereabouts, so Crane and Draper had taken the decision to allow a personal appeal from the parents.

From an Army point of view, they had decided it wouldn't be appropriate for one of those heart wrenching, degrading, open press conferences. That wasn't the Army style, so it had been arranged that one reporter would interview the couple and then that interview would be made available to all the networks for showing on the evening news and breakfast news the following morning. That way the parents could appeal for information on Tyler's whereabouts with dignity, rather than facing a bank of television cameras, photographers and reporters, who would do their best to behave like a baying crowd, winding the parents up until one of them snapped and sobbed and screamed, providing the hysteria they wanted for their news programmes. As Wainwright was military they were hoping for an interview with a bit more decorum.

The local television studios of the BBC weren't what Crane expected. Somehow he expected a studio in a smart purpose built block, with lots of glass and light. But as he and Anderson walked up the road, they were faced with a very ordinary block-built office unit and a very small one at that. As they passed through the reception, they found that other companies occupied the building as well. Making their way to the sixth floor in the lift, the doors opened onto a floor that could be any large open plan office with cubicles, reminding Crane of a challenge maze for laboratory rats.

The receptionist smiled a brilliant white toothed smile, making Crane keep his mouth shut as there was no way his gnashers would match up to the woman, who could easily have been in an advert for cosmetic dentistry. She told them the Wainwrights had already arrived and were in make-up, indicating a sofa against the reception wall where they could wait.

Crane, self conscious in his rumpled raincoat, took it off and slung it over the arm of the settee, then ran a hand over his hair before smoothing down his tie.

"It's alright, Crane," Anderson said, "You're not going on camera," and laughed at his own wit.

"No, I know, but everyone looks so bloody smart."

"Crane, relax, you're the smartest looking man I know. If anyone should be self conscious it's me."

Crane had to agree with Anderson on that. His

tweed jacket was bent and stretched on the sleeves and the back flap creased and crumpled. Whereas Crane had a bright white starched shirt under a freshly cleaned dark suit. His tie was muted and free of food stains.

"I wonder what happens when they're out of make-up?"

As Anderson shook his head to indicate he didn't know, Crane strolled over to the receptionist to find out.

Julie wasn't sure about doing an appeal on television, but desperation had won out. She would do anything to have her child back, so she was being prepared in makeup. Looking at herself in the mirrors, under the harsh light bulbs, she was astonished at the paleness of her skin. She was ghostly white - as though all the blood had drained from her face - and her skin looked paper thin. As she sat there, the makeup artist fussed around her with her pots, powder and paint.

"Is this absolutely necessary?" she asked the woman.

"I'm sorry, Mrs Wainwright, but you have to have makeup on."

"But why? I don't want to look painted, as though I put make up on to go on television. Surely the whole point is my missing child. Not to make me look good on television."

"I know," soothed the woman, "but if you go on television without anything on your skin, you won't show up under the lights, which are even brighter and harsher in the studio than the ones here in the makeup room."

So Julie submitted to having makeup put, on feeling that everything in her life was a compromise. She wanted to scream and shout in rage at the loss of Tyler, but had to behave, be quiet and nod her assent to the makeup.

She was led by the elbow to the television studio by the woman, once she had finished her titivating. Bob was already there, sat on a settee next to the pretty presenter, who looked perfect in every way. Beautiful, thin, wearing gorgeous clothes and the sort of shoes Julie wouldn't be able to walk in, never mind afford to buy. No wonder her husband was smiling so warmly at her.

Crane and Anderson had been led into the studio and told to stand at the back of the control booth, from where they could watch the interview as it was filmed.

He had been surprised when they had been led through the maze of cubicles to an office suite off to one side of the large room which housed the television studio. It appeared that the studio was just another office. They passed through double glass doors into a darkened corridor, from which they were led into the control booth. The lighting was muted in this room, meaning the screens in front of the large audio and video control desk were easy to see and grabbed the eye. Tearing his eyes from the fascinating array of buttons and sliders on the mixing desk, he looked through the glass wall into the studio. Here there were blank walls behind the presenter and Sgt Wainwright. Crane guessed it was so that nothing would take the eye away from the interview when it was shown on television.

Julie Wainwright appeared, looking small and lost, clearly cowed by the experience so far. She reminded Crane of a timid mouse straight out of Beatrix Potter. As she sat next to her husband and put her hands in her lap, Crane could see them trembling even from this distance. He wondered how she would cope when interviewed.

Julie sat next to Bob, who hardly acknowledged her existence, until they were ready to film that was. Then he jumped into concerned husband and father mode, grabbing one of her hands in his and put his arm along the back of the settee behind where she was sitting.

Once the cameras were rolling, Bob talked about wanting to thank the public for all their efforts in trying to find their baby and for getting behind the campaign to find Tyler. He also thanked the military - well he would wouldn't he - and the police.

Then he turned away from Julie, put his arms on his knees and talked directly into the camera. He was clearly born to do this sort of stuff, although she realised that for him it was probably just like briefing his lads about a difficult exercise, where he needed their full co-operation and was trying to get them to work to the best of their ability.

"Someone out there knows what's going on," he said. "Knows where Tyler is. Perhaps saw someone coming home with a baby they didn't have before or heard a baby in the house where previously there wasn't one. Please, everyone, think about your neighbours, people in your block of flats, people in your terrace, people in your street. Is anyone acting suspiciously? Buying baby stuff in the supermarket they've not bought before? The possibilities are endless," he continued, "but I, um we," he glanced at Julie," just want our baby back."

And that's when Julie broke down and cried. She just couldn't help it. It seemed such a daunting prospect, finding Tyler, no wonder the police and the military police hadn't been able to do it.

Asked by the bloody stupid woman presenter how she was feeling, she said, "I just want my baby back. Want to feel her in my arms again. Want to hear her laugh, hear her cry, watch her sleeping. She's my whole world. My reason for living." Julie took a deep breath the way a drowning woman would and then continued, "I want to ask the person who's got her, if she's watching this right now, please think about what you're doing. Think about the heartache you've caused." By now tears were running unchecked down Julie's face. "Can you find it in your heart to return Tyler to her mother? Can you?" she begged.

Appeal

And now to our main story.
The parents of a baby who went missing in Aldershot in
Hampshire have made an emotional appeal for her return.

Kim Symmonds turned off the television with tears in her eyes. She could only imagine what Julie Wainwright was going through. As if the poor woman didn't have enough stress and worry in her life from being a soldier's wife, before all this happened. No wonder Julie was close to collapse.

Since being married, Kim was beginning to see that wives like Julie Wainwright should matter to the British Army more than they did. They were the ones who engendered hope, courage and commitment in the soldiers sent away to fight for their country, as well as their military leaders. If only these women were rewarded by officialdom with the respect and dignity they deserved. Looking at Army life from the other side of the fence was causing Kim to have a completely different perspective on life in the forces than when she was a serving soldier. She was now in the unique position of understanding the point of view of those in the Army, as well as those out of the Army.

She'd seen firsthand, through Julie Wainwright, how debilitating loss is. How it is so hard to handle. But that went for any woman dealing with loss. The loss of a child, brother or husband. And that loss didn't necessarily mean death. The loss of their husband through divorce affected women badly. Shattered their confidence, made them emotionally unbalanced and sometimes unable to participate fully in life. Becoming a mere bystander.

She wondered how the mothers of the boys who had given their lives for their country were coping with their loss. What strategies they had for coming to terms with it. Did they ever come to terms with it, or were they left frozen in time, unable to move along in their lives? She wasn't advocating that they should forget their lost one, but wondered if, somehow, they could move forward with the positivity of that love walking along beside them.

Kim sat on the settee thinking, as her cup of coffee went cold on the table. Speculating how best she could serve her husband, the soldiers and, just maybe, the army of wives stationed on Aldershot Garrison. Turning over the possibilities in her mind. Examining each idea and either keeping it for further consideration, or discarding it.

Kerry was over the moon with the reborn Tyler. Not only did the child breathe and curl her hand around Kerry's finger, but she cried and was pacified with a dummy. She proudly showed Tyler off to the Mollies and Alan.

"Isn't she beautiful?" she asked Alan, hoping he'd feel the same about the reborn Tyler as she did. "Look, feel her skin, it's so soft to the touch and warm, just like a baby's should be."

Kerry knew Alan had trouble moving his arms, so she gently took one of his poor deformed hands and stroked it along Tyler's arm, so he could feel the child's soft skin too. He'd lost three fingers on one hand and two on the other. But it didn't seem to bother Alan, he just sat stoically in his chair, placidly watching Kerry as she bustled around looking after their family.

"I think I'll leave her in the playpen, Alan," she said. "I've cleaned it all out with disinfectant and there's only a very slight mark now on the bottom of it."

She put Tyler in the playpen and surrounded her with her toys. Kerry was delighted when Tyler's hand curled around her favourite teething ring.

"Did you see that, Alan? Tyler's so glad to be back with us, I'm sure of it."

Kerry stopped fussing over the baby and sat on the couch looking at Alan. After a pause she said, "Of course I've remembered to cover the hinge bit of the bar. What do you think I am, stupid? Now look, stop trying to ruin our happy family time. I know, I'll put the news on, you always like watching that, don't you?" and Kerry switched on the TV turning it to the news channel.

Kerry sat back to watch as well, thinking that she deserved a bit of a rest herself.

"And now to our main story," the presenter said. "The parents of a child who went missing in Aldershot in Hampshire have made an emotional appeal for her return."

"Oh look, Alan," Kerry called to him. "This bit's about Aldershot, how exciting, we're never normally in the news. Yes I know we live in North Camp now, but we used to live in Aldershot and anyway it's only a few minutes' walk to Aldershot, so stop splitting hairs."

Kerry turned her attention to the screen once more, where a couple, clearly very distressed were talking to the camera.

"My goodness me! It's Julie Wainwright, Alan. You know, the one I've told you about before. The one from the mother and baby group. You know, Tyler's mother."

Kerry was fascinated by the way Julie looked. Her short trendy haircut was no longer artistically sculpted around her face, but was so dull and lifeless that it looked like the woman was wearing a synthetic wig.

Her husband, Bob, who Kerry had never met, was looking angry rather than upset. His jaw was clenched to match his fists and he was staring into the camera as though he could see through it, all the way to Kerry in her flat in North Camp. She shrunk back into the settee to get away from the vehement anger emanating from him.

"Alan, stop chattering for a moment, I can't hear what they're saying."

"Please, please, don't hurt my child," Julie Wainwright was saying. "She must be very upset and frightened and needs her mother. I just want my baby back. Want to feel her in my arms again. Want to hear her laugh, hear her cry, watch her sleeping. She's my whole world. My reason for living. I want to ask the person who's got her, if she's watching this right now, please think about what you're doing. Think about the heartache you've caused. Can you find it in your heart to return Tyler to her mother? Can you?"

Kerry heard the final muffled words before Julie began sobbing uncontrollably.

"Oh my goodness, Alan. They want Tyler back. Julie

seems very upset doesn't she? But the question is - do they deserve to get her back? What do you think?"

Second Chance

"Well, I'm not so sure, Alan," Kerry said, picking Tyler from the playpen and balancing her on her knee. "After all, Julie did leave Tyler alone in the pram that day."

Kerry fussed over the child and smoothed down her beautiful brown curly hair.

"That scream was heartbreaking and the only one who gave a damn was me," Kerry reminded Alan. "No one else even looked into the pram. That scream was for me to find her. I'm sure of it."

Tyler started crying, so Kerry popped the magnetic dummy into her mouth.

"There, there, Tyler," she soothed, "there's nothing to worry about. Just look at that, Alan, just the thought of going back has made Tyler cry."

Julie put the child in the crook of her arm and started to rock her.

"Of course I saw how upset Julie was, Alan. I'm not sure about that husband of hers though, he looked a bit mean to me and I don't want Tyler going back to someone who is mean and horrible."

Kerry got up and started to walk around the cramped flat as she listened to Alan.

"Alright," she said, "Maybe he's just angry because Tyler's missing, not because he'd get angry with the child. Mind you, the last time I talked to Julie she said that Bob wasn't much of a father."

Kerry went to get a bottle of formula from the fridge and boiled the kettle for hot water to heat it with and continued to listen to Alan.

"I suppose you've got a point there," Kerry conceded. "Fathers are different from mothers." Then she laughed. "You're right when you say soldiers are different from civilian men. They find it harder to express their true emotions."

The kettle had boiled so Kerry put some hot water into a jug and placed the formula bottle carefully in it.

"Julie did say at one point," she continued, "that she thought Bob was having an affair. Surely that's not good behaviour. Maybe he's planning on leaving Julie for another woman and then Tyler would be going back to a single mother and trust me, I know how hard that is. She wouldn't even have you for help and advice like I have. But then again perhaps it's just the Army that's Bob's other woman. Really the Army is worse than another woman. It is a soldier's controller, his dictator. The Army owns him. I'm sure Julie's husband spends more time with the Army than with her. Just like you did. Remember?"

Tyler started crying again, so Kerry tested the temperature of the formula on the back of her hand and carried the bottle and the baby back to the settee.

Once Tyler was feeding happily Kerry said, "You're right, Alan. Everyone does deserve a second chance. I'm sure Julie will never leave Tyler alone again like she did. I expect she's learned her lesson. Understands now that there's nothing as precious as a child and you must put them first all the time. Oh look, Tyler's fast asleep now."

Julie took away the bottle. "She's not taken much milk, mind. I expect it was the shock of seeing her mum on television. I'll just put her down."

Kerry carefully laid Kerry on her back in the playpen.

"No," she said to Alan as she straightened up, "I don't want to call the police. They won't understand. I want to see Julie and give Tyler back myself. Make sure she understands why I did what I did. And that she's got to change her behaviour in the future. I'll talk to that Padre Symmonds. I'm sure he'll help. Arrange it so we can meet up. After all he was so good when I left Molly on his church steps. He said those nice things in the newspaper, remember?"

Kerry walked over to the computer.

"What? What's his phone number? I don't know but I'm sure it'll be on the internet. Everything usually is."

30

Kim was on her own in the house. She wandered into the kitchen to make a coffee and then back to the lounge again. Wondered when Francis would be home, as he was due back with his Unit today. He hadn't given a specific time, just said that he'd be home late.

Sitting there, alone, she realised she was basically a single woman and would be for the rest of their married life and a single parent, if they ever had children.

They had talked about this before they got married and again since, so Kim was able to take strength from the knowledge that Francis loved her and was still thinking of her, whilst he was away. She had to trust Francis implicitly, as she wouldn't know where he was, or who he was with, many, many times over the course of their marriage. She was secure in the knowledge that he felt the same about her as she did him, but was under no illusion that essentially she was embarking on a long distance relationship. Plus the fact that there were normally three people in an Army marriage; the wife, the husband and the Army. Because, of course, a soldier is married to the Army as much, if not more, than to his wife. Kim was an exception to that rule, for she had four people in her marriage. For Francis was a man of God as well as a soldier and a married man.

She knew her prior experience and knowledge of the Army way of life was crucial in her understanding of Army marriages. Enabling her to go into her relationship with her 'eyes wide open' as it were. But how many Army wives had her background and knowledge? Very few. Of that she was certain. Which meant she could be in a unique position to help. Help the wives understand that the Army is their husband's 'other woman'. That the Army is a controller, who their husband will spend more time with than his wife. That the Army is a dictator, who expects - and gets - blind obedience.

Would she be able to listen to their anger and help them channel it into the energy they need to look after their family, effectively alone? Would it be possible to encourage and help the wives be strong until their husband returned? And then when he does return, be understanding enough to give him time to bring himself back emotionally from whatever horror he saw whilst he was away? The men needed that space, before they could rejoin their families in mind as well as in body.

It was clear to Kim that someone in this role would be a great asset to Francis. The only real question therefore was - could that someone be her? And what would be the best way to proceed? She couldn't just go around blindly offering platitudes. She wanted her help to be on a more professional basis, to make sure she didn't do more harm than good.

The incessant ringing of the telephone dragged her back from her deliberations. Distracted and a bit annoyed, Kim grabbed the receiver. "Hello?" she barked, as though she were still a soldier.

"Is the Padre there?" a woman's voice asked.

"No," Kim moderated her voice, I'm sorry, he's away today. Can I take a message?" and Kim pulled towards her the notepad and pen she always kept by the phone.

"Oh, well, alright, I suppose. It's just that I want to give the baby back."

Kim froze, pen half way to the paper. "The baby?" she managed, shock seriously hampering her ability to speak.

"Yes, you know the one that's missing.

"Yes, of course, I do. Tyler."

"That's right. Well I want to give her back to her parents. We've decided to give them a second chance. But I'll only do it if Padre Symmonds is there, as he'll be able to make them understand."

Kim's questions tumbled out, "Second chance? Understand what? When? What's your name? How's Tyler?"

But Kerry ignored them all and said, "Is he there today?"

Kim swallowed before answering, "No I'm sorry, he'll be back late tonight. But I'm his wife. I could meet you if you like?"

"No. No. It must be the Padre. Tell him I'll come tomorrow. About 2 o'clock. To the church. Bye."

"No wait!" Kim called, but the line was dead in her hand. Quickly pressing the button to cut the line, she lifted her finger and as soon as she got the dialling tone, she rang 1471 in an attempt to get the telephone number of the person who had just called her. But it wasn't available. The caller had blocked the number before making the call.

31

"You've just done what?" Crane couldn't quite take in what Kim had just told him on the telephone.

"I've just spoken to a woman who told me she had Tyler and that she wants to hand her over to the Wainwrights. As soon as the call ended I wrote down what she said, pretty much verbatim, before I forgot it."

"Bloody well done, Kim. Can you come into the office?"

"Of course, sir."

"Crane, or Tom, to you now, Kim. I'm no longer your boss."

"Sorry, force of habit," Kim laughed

Crane replaced the receiver but continued to look at the telephone in astonishment. After all that effort, someone rang out of the blue, just like that. Or maybe it wasn't just like that. After all it was only yesterday that the Wainwright's had made their appeal. It had been shown on the national news programmes last night and on the breakfast shows this morning. So perhaps, just perhaps, the appeal had actually worked.

Shaking himself out of his stupor, Crane grabbed the phone and called Anderson and Draper, then strode out of his office to find Billy.

They were all embroiled in a powwow. Crane, Draper, Anderson, Billy and Kim. All had agreed that it was entirely possible the person who had Tyler was Kerry. However, they felt they couldn't possibly interfere and go to her flat and confront her. As Draper put it, what if it all went wrong? If Kerry felt threatened, surrounded or cornered and if she did have Tyler, the baby could end up getting harmed. No one was willing to take that risk.

"Do you mind telling us again what the caller said about *deserve another chance*, please, Kim?" Crane asked.

Kim took a moment to find the passage and then said, "*I want to give her back to her parents. We've decided to give them a second chance. But I'll only do it if Padre Symmonds is there, as he'll be able to make them understand.*"

"*We've decided.* Who the hell is we? If it is Kerry, she lives on her own."

"That could be a pointer that is isn't Kerry, then," said Anderson. "Was there any sign of a second person living in her flat?"

"No, not that I can recall. Can you Billy?"

"No, boss, there was a picture of her husband and some of his stuff on her dressing table in the bedroom. I also noticed she was wearing his dog tags around her neck. I suppose she could be talking about the 'royal we' as it were, you know, talking as though her husband were still alive and they'd decided together."

"What about this *second chance*? What's that all about?" Crane was still perplexed.

"Perhaps she thought Julie wasn't a good enough mother, by leaving the child outside the shop," said Kim. "She could have thought that Julie had abandoned her child, if you try and think about it from the point of view of a warped mind that is."

"Do you think that's why she took the baby?" Draper looked astonished. "Because she thought the mother wasn't looking after her properly? And that she could do a better job?" Draper seemed to involuntarily shudder at the thought, Crane noticed.

"Well, whatever the reasons, if it is Kerry, she is clearly not in her right mind. If we're not going into her flat, then we'll put her under surveillance. From now until 14:00 hours tomorrow afternoon. Let's see if she leaves the flat and if she does, perhaps we can confirm that she's got Tyler."

"Agreed," said Draper. Although Crane didn't really want his agreement or his approval, as he was going to do it anyway.

Carrying on with what he was going to say before Draper interrupted him Crane said, "As Kerry knows Billy and I, it better not be us. Derek, how are your lot fixed for a bit of surveillance?"

"Not a chance, Crane. Can some of your RMPs do it? We've been so stretched with the search over the past couple of weeks, I don't even think I've got any officers who could stay awake long enough to watch a flat."

"Alright, Derek, I'll get Staff Sgt Jones to do it."

"Not a couple of corporals?"

"No, I won't trust anyone other than Jones. This job's too important."

"Right, Crane, get it all organised and keep me posted," Draper said as he got up and nodded to everyone before walking out in the direction of his office.

Crane got ready to go and see Jones, who he knew

was as tired as the rest of them, but wouldn't shirk away from the importance of the surveillance, once it had been explained to him.

"Anderson and I will come over and see the Padre when he's back, later this evening. Is that alright?" Crane asked Kim. "We'll want to discuss with both of you the best way to handle the handover of the child."

"Of course, s…, sorry, Crane," and Kim left the office, blushing, trying to hide her pink face behind her hair.

Crane smiled as she left and then turned to Anderson and Billy. "Down to business, then," and he almost rubbed his hands in glee, but managed to stop himself in time. He was so relieved that it looked like they were going to achieve the safe return of baby Tyler. And as a result of that they could get back to planning and co-ordinating the drugs arrests at last. For once Tyler was back, Wainwright would be able to hand the drugs to Josip Anic.

32

Kim's text message to Francis meant he went straight home after he returned from exercise, rather than going to the Mess with his colleagues. 'Come straight home' was the instruction, so he obeyed it like a good husband and soldier. Wondering what Kim could have in store for him, he pulled up onto the drive, bundled his kit out of the boot and crashed through the front door to be greeted by a very serious looking trio - Kim, Crane and DI Anderson.

"Hey, what are you two doing in my house," he called to Crane and Anderson, as he went over to kiss Kim. "Have I done something wrong? In that case it's a fair cop!" he joked and held up his wrists for the handcuffs. But he soon realised his joke had fallen flat as all three continued to look at him without a smile between them and so he dropped into a chair. "What is it? What's happened?"

As Kim relayed the phone call from an unknown woman, but who it was thought was Kerry Chandler, Francis' expression matched that of his colleagues.

"Oh my," he said. "Do you think Tyler's okay?"

"Sorry, sir, but we have no way of knowing," and to

the Padre's incredulity Crane gave him the background they had on Kerry Chandler.

"So let me get this straight," Francis attempted to summarise the situation. "I'm to meet a woman, believed to be Kerry Chandler, at 14:00 hours tomorrow at the Garrison Church, with Julie and Bob Wainwright. The woman will then return Tyler to the Wainwrights. But Kerry is also believed to be the mother of the dead baby left at the church a while ago. And not forgetting that there may be a reborn doll that looks incredibly lifelike in the mix somewhere."

"That's about right, sir," agreed DI Anderson. "So you see this has to be handled very carefully indeed."

"Yes, I can certainly see that. Oh thanks, love," he said to Kim as she placed a steaming cup of coffee in his hand. "How did she sound on the telephone?" he asked Kim.

"Perfectly normal really," she replied. "Or at least she didn't sound crazy, if that's what you mean."

"I suppose it is, but who's to say what crazy sounds like? At least she sounded rational."

"I guess," Kim said, frowning as though trying to recall the voice in her head. "She was certainly talking normally at any rate."

"So, the question really is, do you feel you are able to meet with her, Padre?" Crane said. "Obviously we'll be in the background, somewhere she can't see us. But it means you could be in a vulnerable position for a while, with the Wainwrights and Kerry in the same room and the baby between them. I'll be having a stern word with Bob Wainwright to make sure his anger doesn't get the better of him and he kicks off - with what could be dire consequences."

"You mean Kerry could harm the baby?" For the

first time Francis really understood the implications of his facilitating the meeting.

"Or Wainwright could harm Kerry if there's something wrong with the baby, but by that time we'll be right outside the door. We'll be able to step in, don't worry, sir."

But Francis was worried, or rather very concerned, by the responsibility this Kerry woman had put upon him and he got very little sleep that night, spending most of it talking things through with Kim. Her cool, calm, support meant a great deal to him and he was seriously beginning to wonder how he ever did his job properly without her.

For Bob Wainwright things were definitely looking up. He could get rid of the drugs in his garage at last. As their baby was to be returned tomorrow at 14:00 hours, he contacted Josip Anic. For once the call made by Bob, rather than Anic pestering him at least once a day.

"About bloody time," was the growl from Anic. If Bob expected pleasantness and praise, he certainly didn't get it from the Croatian.

"Look, because of the hand over by this woman tomorrow," Bob had completely forgotten to watch what he was saying, "the police eyes have moved away from us and they are all concentrating on the church and some bint call Kerry. So, for once I can get out somewhere other than the bloody office, without beady eyes on me. Where do you want to meet tomorrow morning?"

After he had been given instructions, Bob shut his mobile phone and took a great lungful of cigarette smoke. As he exhaled, he felt the tension drain from his body. He wasn't worried about the hand over, he was sure he'd get his money and then all their financial problems would be solved. Julie had no idea how badly off they were. He'd managed to keep from her the fact that they had regularly been spending more money each month than he earned in his salary. And then there'd been all the expense of the baby. It meant that he'd been caught out and the credit cards and store cards, all six of them, were now maxed out with little hope of paying them off without the drugs money. And thank God no one had searched his garage. In fact a Military Police jeep that had been parked in front of his garage for the past two weeks, had kept the drugs nice and safe. That had also gone today, meaning he was free to complete the transaction.

As he walked back into the house, his mind was entirely focused on the drugs and the money, with no space left in his head for thoughts about the safe, or otherwise, return of his daughter.

The Return

Kerry settled herself carefully into the back of the taxi. She'd arranged with the Padre's wife to hand Tyler back today, but she couldn't remember what time they'd agreed. But Kerry didn't think it mattered. She was ready, so she decided to go. Alan had been a bit upset to see Tyler leave them, but Kerry reminded him they still had the Mollies, so not to worry and that seemed to cheer him up. They still had a lot to do looking after two children, she'd told him.

Tyler was happily settled in the baby carrier, which Kerry had strapped around her and put the baby in. Then she put her coat on, deciding on the one she had when she was pregnant, as it was nice and big and covered the child as well as herself, so Tyler wouldn't get cold.

After paying the driver, Kerry climbed out of the taxi and walked up to the church. Putting her hand on the door handle, she found it was unlocked and the old hinges creaked as she pushed it open. The church seemed to be empty, so Kerry walked around it, fascinated by all the flags hanging from the walls. They were regimental flags and Kerry was looking for Alan's regiment, when a man walked in.

"Good morning," he called, "can I help at all?"

"Oh, morning," Kerry said, "I was just looking for my husband's regimental flag, but I can't seem to see it."

"Who is he with? Oh, sorry, I'm Padre Symmonds," he introduced himself and held out his hand.

"I thought it must be you," Kerry said, shaking the Padre's hand and then pulling it away to wrap her arms around Tyler. "I've come to see you about Tyler. I talked to your wife on the phone yesterday. What a lovely lady she is. Do you know she offered to meet me herself? I hope she didn't mind that I wanted you to help, not her. Is Julie here yet?" Kerry asked, all thoughts of Regimental flags gone.

"Um, no, not yet. Would you like a coffee while we wait?"

"Thank you. I hope they won't be long, Tyler is sleeping at the moment, but she'll want feeding soon. Why don't you give them a ring and tell them I'm here."

"What an excellent suggestion - I'm sorry I don't know your name? Let's go through to my office."

Kerry told the Padre her name and then followed him through the echoing church into his office. She could hear a phone ringing in the distance, but he made no move to rush through the church to answer it. He seemed a bit nervous, she thought, as he kept turning round to check she was following him and also looking around the church to see if anyone else was there. When they got to his office, she sat in the proffered chair, but refused to give up the child when the Padre suggested she might be more comfortable if she took the baby sling off.

"No thank you, Padre," she said primly, "Tyler is quite happy here," and she encircled the baby in her arms. "So, if you wouldn't mind, can you ring them? I want them both here mind. I want you to make them understand that they must listen to you about being better parents. They've been a bit lapse in their parenting of Tyler, what with Julie leaving her alone outside the shop like that and Bob not really being interested in the baby. I know that's true," she quickly said as she saw the Padre look at her incredulously. "Julie told me herself. In fact she was so upset about Bob never being there, she thought he was having an affair. So, really, he must understand now that his family comes first. I want to know they've learned their lesson."

She watched as Padre Symmonds grabbed the phone on his desk, dropping it in his haste, before righting it and dialling a number from memory.

"Ah, good morning," he said when the phone must have been answered, "Padre Symmonds here. Yes, yes I am ringing with good news. Kerry is here already." He paused listening to the person on the other end. "Yes, Tyler is with her, so can everyone come as soon as possible?"

Kerry thought he seemed very grateful as he gabbled, "Oh good, thanks a lot, yes, yes, see you soon," before putting the phone down. Maybe he was just excited for Julie and Bob, she decided.

He got up from behind his desk and said, "Right, time for coffee I think. Um, before I make it, can I see the baby?"

"Of course," Kerry said, opening her coat a little to expose Tyler's head with those beautiful brown curls in her hair. Tyler had her dummy in her mouth and her eyes were closed in sleep. "There she is. Isn't she lovely?"

"Beautiful," agreed the Padre and put his hand out towards the baby.

33

Padre Symmonds was stunned when he realised his visitor was Kerry, who had arrived at 10.30 hours in the morning instead of 14:00 hours in the afternoon. Not wanting to take his attention from Kerry, he'd phoned Kim and trusted her to ring Crane, Anderson and the Wainwrights.

He wasn't at all sure what Kerry was on about, when she said wanted him to talk to the Wainwrights about parenting, but he'd do whatever he had to do to make sure the baby was returned to her parents. From what he could see, Tyler was fine. She appeared to be breathing, as the child's chest was rising and falling. She had a dummy in her mouth and occasionally emitted a weak cry. When he'd reached out a hand to touch the child, though, Kerry had reacted as though she'd been stung and pushed back into her chair, moving the child out of his reach. So he'd had to let go of the idea of taking Tyler from Kerry and had no choice but to settle back and wait for help to arrive.

Crane was pretty sure he had everything covered. Jones was watching Kerry's flat. Anderson was watching Josip

Anic and Crane was watching Bob Wainwright. He'd just spoken to Jones, who'd confirmed that Kerry was still in her flat.

Last night, once Kerry's lights had gone out, Jones had been relieved during midnight and 07:00 hours. It was a good job, Jones had told Crane, because he was beginning to see double, he was that tired. He'd spent the past couple of weeks organising the Army contingent part of the searches. Working 18 hour days. Seven days a week. No one had wanted to give up hope. No one had wanted to stop working, to stop looking. No one wanted Tyler found in a part of the search area they'd been responsible for and missed her. They'd beaten and bashed every tree, bush and plant they could find on Ash Ranges, around Farnborough airport and all other Army land between here and the coast. All to no avail.

The trouble was, the relief they all felt with the realisation that the case could be coming to a successful conclusion, had hit home and they were beginning to relax. Which was a very dangerous thing to do. Relaxing made them realise how tired they were. The adrenaline leaving their bodies and leaving them all drained.

So Crane was geeing up the troops this morning. Keeping everyone on their guard. Making sure they were wide awake and ready for anything. For anything could happen. Especially something they hadn't prepared for.

Crane himself was sat with Billy in a car, parked in a side road, from where they had a line of sight to the side of Wainwright's house. They were to follow him wherever he went. Be it to work, out shopping or to take the drugs to Anic. Crane was hoping for the latter.

Crane was looking down at the packet of cigarettes

he was fumbling with, wondering how many he had left and whether he'd have enough to keep him going until he could get to the shop, when Billy said, "Something's up, boss. Bob's just come out of the house."

He watched as the man went to the garage, lifted the large metal door and disappeared inside. Billy made sure he was filming and a few minutes later Wainwright emerged with several boxes that he packed into the boot of his car. He did that three times. Then walked back into the house, after carefully locking his vehicle.

Crane grabbed his phone and called Anderson, who was clearly pleased to hear that Wainwright was getting ready to move the drugs.

"Looks like the hand over might be at the Body Shop, then," he told Crane. "Anic's on the move now and heading in that direction, so no doubt I'll see you over there later on."

When they'd sketched out their plan of action last night, they'd decided to let Wainwright deliver the drugs, get paid and return home. Once Wainwright was out of the way, Anderson would arrest Anic. After the handover of baby Tyler, Wainwright would then be arrested.

It looked to Crane that this could be a very good day. A very good day indeed. And then his mobile rang.

Bob Wainwright walked back into the house. He'd made three trips from the metal cabinet in the garage, to the boot of his car, and now all the drugs were stored safely in there.

"Right, Julie," he called from the hall. "I'm off now!"

"Bob, Bob," she called and ran out from the kitchen. "Where the hell are you going?" She had been wiping her hands on a towel and flicked it over her shoulder.

"You know where. I told you last night."

"Oh yes, to see that gangster and give him your filthy drugs," and she looked at him with scorn turning her face ugly.

"Look, we've been through this before. I've tried to tell you we need the money, but you're not taking it in."

"No, Bob, I'm not taking it in. I'm not taking anything else in other than what's happening about Tyler."

"Well, that's bloody obvious. Anyway you're getting her back today, so what's your problem?"

"I'm getting her back? We're getting her back. Or have you forgotten that you're her father?"

"For God's sake, woman. What's the matter with you? Of course I know she's my daughter!"

"Well you could show it. By staying home with me sometimes. Don't you think I need you? I could do with some support here!"

"You, you, you, that's all I bloody hear in this house. I'm doing this for YOU, you stupid cow. You and our daughter. Now let me go and get rid of this lot, collect the money and then this afternoon we can both go and pick up Tyler. Think about it. Once she's back we'll have the police crawling all over us again. Surely you don't want them to find the drugs in the garage."

His frustration with his mealy mouthed wife threatened to spill over into anger, so he took a step back from her before he did something he'd regret. Having had enough of trying to make Julie see sense, he turned to leave the house. And then his mobile phone rang.

34

It was Jones ringing Crane's mobile, reporting that Kerry was on the move. She'd come out of the flats with what looked like a bundle strapped to her chest, partially covered by a coat. It looked as though it could be Tyler in a baby carrier.

"So what are you doing?" Crane asked.

"Following her taxi. I'm a few cars back, but to be honest she seems pretty oblivious to everything around her. She is keeping her attention focused on the child in the carrier, if that's what it actually is."

"Which direction are you going in?"

"Towards the Garrison, so maybe she's heading for the church. Looks like she could have decided to turn up early."

"Early is an understatement, Jones. I'll tell the others. Keep me posted," said Crane and quickly ended the call, anxious to speak to Anderson, Padre Symmonds and the Wainwrights, to let them know Kerry was on the move and to insist they all stay in position for now, or at least until Jones reported back.

Crane's call had caught Wainwright leaving his house and he could see the man talking to him on his mobile.

Crane was enjoying himself, finding it amusing that Wainwright had no idea Crane was watching him.

"What do you mean she's on the move?" Wainwright demanded, in a tone Crane felt bordered on insubordination. After all Crane was of superior rank, being a Sgt Major whereas Wainwright was merely a Sergeant. But for the moment he let that pass.

"All I know right now is that she's in a taxi heading in the direction of the Garrison. Where are you?" Crane asked.

"At home, but I was just going out. I was on my way to the car." Crane could hear a petulant whine in Wainwright's voice.

"Well, as of now, you're not going anywhere, so bloody well go back indoors and wait for my call."

Crane punched the call end button and watched Wainwright standing on his driveway. He looked at his phone as though he wanted to throw it far away, then clenched his jaw and put the phone back in his pocket. Shaking his head he moved away from his car and back into the house.

"I know how you feel, mate," Crane said to Wainwright's retreating back and proceeded to speak to Anderson, who Billy had just raised.

"Jesus Christ," blasphemed Anderson. "You can't trust women. Looks like I'm going to be left out on a limb with Anic and his money, but no drugs."

"I know, Derek, but we have to be cautious and careful. Jones is following Kerry, but we don't know if this is a ruse, if it's real and she has the baby or if she's on her way to collect her. I can't authorise picking her up now. What if she's not got the baby with her and won't tell us where she is? Sorry, Derek, I just can't risk it and you know it."

"Alright, alright, it's just so bloody frustrating, that's all. Let me know when you hear anything," and Anderson cleared the line.

Crane was just picking up his mobile to call Padre Symmonds when it rang. Looking at the display he saw it was Kim. At the same time the radio buzzed and Crane indicated that Billy should answer it.

"Morning, sir," Kim said in Crane's ear. "The Padre has just called me to say Kerry is sat in his office and that they are both waiting for the Wainwrights to come and collect Tyler."

Despite the seriousness of the message, it still struck Crane as interesting that Kim had fallen back on her military training in a time of crisis. He opened his mouth to reply when Billy touched him on the arm and interrupted him. Asking Kim to hold on, he listened to Billy.

"Boss, Jones has just said Kerry's at the Garrison church."

"That's just what Kim has told me, hang on, Billy, while I speak to Kim. Did he say anything about the baby, or Kerry?" he asked Kim, switching his attention back to her. "What's her mood, do you know?"

"Sorry, sir, he didn't manage to give me any information other than she was there and waiting for the Wainwrights."

"Very well, thanks, Kim. You can call and tell him we'll be there as soon as possible."

Turning to Billy he said, "Inform Anderson that it looks like he won't get the drugs hand over he was so looking forward to after all. I'm going to tell Bob and Julie what's happened and then I'll go to the church in their car. I want the car with the drugs in where we can see it. You follow behind us. Oh, and you better let

Draper know what's going on as well."

"Okay, boss," and Billy reached for the radio as Crane left the car and sprinted over to the Wainwright's house, his coat billowing behind him in the wind.

35

Furious just didn't cover the way Bob Wainwright was feeling right at that moment, after Crane told him over the phone that the stupid cow Kerry was at the Garrison Church with their daughter. Because mingled in with the fury was fear on two fronts. Fear that Anic would actually kill him if he didn't get his drugs that morning and fear that if he wasn't careful he wouldn't get his daughter back.

But to be honest on a scale of one to ten, he was more frightened of Anic than he was of his wife, or of not getting his daughter back. He knew he shouldn't feel that way. Should be more concerned about the return of his daughter. But if he was honest with himself, the job had always come first for him. The job being the Army, his lads and his regiment. That had always come first before his family. And an extension of that job was his extracurricular activities, such as the drugs deal with Anic.

But then he saw Julie's face when he told her it appeared Kerry was on her way to the church with Tyler. Early. Julie literally collapsed in front of him. She crumpled to the floor and began sobbing.

"Pull yourself together, Julie," he said looming over her and reaching down to pull her onto her feet.

"Oh, Bob, I can't believe it," she said, leaning against him and turning her tear stained face to his. "I've been so frightened. Frightened that we'd never find Tyler. Or if we did, that she'd be, she'd, be…"

Bob didn't give Julie a chance to complete her sentence. "Well it seems she's alive, so you don't need to worry anymore. But what about Anic?" he said. "What the fuck am I going to do about him? He's the one we should be worried about now!"

"Anic!" Julie screamed. "How can you think about Anic at a time like this? You fucking heartless bastard," and she pulled away from him.

"You don't bloody understand, do you?" Now it was his turn to shout. "You have no idea what Anic is like and what he could do to me if he doesn't get his drugs. I swear he's one of the most dangerous men I've ever met."

"Here we go again," she said. "Me, me, me. It's always, me, with you, isn't it Bob? Well for once this is about your family. About Tyler and me. And you better bloody put us first this time."

Bob knew she was right and was desperately trying to work out how to play this. He'd have to get hold of Anic right now. Before they left for the church.

"Alright, alright," he said to Julie. "Don't go on. Of course we'll go to the church. But first I've got to make a call," and he pulled out his phone and speed dialled Anic's number.

As the man answered, Wainwright said without preamble, "I'm going to have to come later today. Something's come up that I can't get out of."

The roar of rage surging through the phone made

Bob hold the mobile away from his ear. As he did so, he heard a voice behind him say, "I hope you don't mind, but I let myself in."

Wainwright whirled around and saw Crane leaning against the door. He had no idea how long the investigator had been standing there. No idea how much Crane had heard of his conversation with Julie, or his phone call with Anic.

"It's just that Padre Symmonds' wife has called," Crane continued, shouting over the swearing coming out of Bob's mobile. "Kerry has arrived at the church with Tyler and she's insisting that you both meet her there. Apparently she has something she wants to say to you."

"What?" blustered Bob, quickly closing his mobile to cut Anic off and stuffing the phone in his pocket. "What does she want to say?"

"Damned if I know, but that's the message. Sorry to interrupt your phone call. Do you want to call whoever it was back?"

As Bob shook his head, Crane smiled and said, "Alright then, shall we go? Oh, by the way, can we go in your car, Bob? Sgt Williams has mine."

Bob didn't fall for the innocent look on Crane's face. At that moment he knew he was finished. The realisation slammed into him, that the Branch had been watching him all along, and he took an involuntary step backwards. They hadn't stood down as he originally thought. He saw the sly smile on Crane's face and was convinced that Crane knew about the drugs in his car. Whichever way he looked at it he was royally fucked. He had no choice but to go to the church. In his own car. With the drugs in it. With Crane. Whatever happened, if they got Tyler back or not, he realised that he wouldn't be returning home afterwards with Julie. Still, he supposed, at least in military police custody he'd be safe from Anic. Unless, of course, they released him to the Aldershot civilian police. At that thought a shudder ran down his back. He'd be close to Anic at the police station, for the police would surely be arresting Anic as well. To see what they could get him for.

"Ready?" Crane asked him, still holding his gaze.

"Ready," agreed Wainwright and he pulled his car keys out of his pocket, knowing that Crane must be able to see the culpability written all over his face.

36

"I should have bloody known something would go wrong," said Anderson into his mobile phone. "Should have known catching Anic red handed was nothing more than a pipe dream."

"Come on, sir, it's not that bad," Billy's voice sounded tinny over the mobile phone. "The boss said that if we work on Wainwright, we'll get him to confirm that Anic was going to be the purchaser of his drugs from Afghanistan. I'm sure we can entice him to talk by cutting him a deal if he co-operates."

"You better be right," Anderson sighed. "I'll let you know what's going on at this end, give you a shout when we've arrested Anic. Tell Crane the only thing I can think of is to arrest him for conspiracy to purchase and distribute a Class A drug. Which I guess could be a whole lot of nothing. Anic can afford the best solicitors and barristers, you know, so I wouldn't hold your breath if I was you. I'm certainly not."

He cut the call and mumbled a few choice words to himself. After contacting his team by radio to advise them Wainwright wouldn't be showing up, he told them to hold their positions while he worked out what to do.

He swept his eyes over the industrial unit that housed Anic's motor body repair shop. There was a large parking area in front of the unit which was clear of vehicles and there were two beefy looking minders positioned at either side of the large open door. He radioed to the team who had eyes on the unit and could see into the repair shop itself.

"Can you see where Anic is?"

"In the office at the back of the unit, Guv," came the reply.

"Mmm, I need him out in the open really. Hold your position."

"Guv," the officer confirmed.

The teams Anderson had with him were from the local Armed Response Unit and the Serious Organised Crime Unit, who Anderson had been liaising closely with, as they tracked Anic's movements and worked out his business dealings and organisational structure. But Anderson knew that this was his last chance of being involved with any investigation into Anic. All future cases would be dealt with by the newly formed National Crime Agency, "the British FBI" as it was already being dubbed by the media and local officers. So Anderson really wanted this last chance to bring the Croatian to justice, before all his files were handed over to the NCA, and he once more swore out his frustration.

His main concern was arresting everyone without any injuries to either his team or Anic's men. He was worried about going in while Anic was holed up in his office. The Croatian could decide to make a stand if he was armed and angry enough and barricade himself in his office. That would not constitute 'coming quietly' as far as Anderson was concerned. It wouldn't be the sensible thing to do, but Anderson didn't think Anic was in the least bit sensible. His track record proved that he used force rather than diplomacy in his dealings with people and Anderson couldn't take a chance on Anic actually showing any glimmer of rationality when put under pressure.

Anderson had teams concealed on either side of the unit, as well as the front and the back of it and was just working on a ploy to get Anic outside in the car park, when he heard a roar of anger coming from the body shop.

"All units make ready. Anic could be on the move," Anderson whispered into his radio and heard in his imagination the clicks of all the sniper rifles, semi-automatic guns and small firearms being cocked and made ready.

Just then Anic appeared at the front door of the unit, shouting and gesticulating. He seemed to be issuing orders to the several men that had emerged from nowhere and were now surrounding him. Anderson put his binoculars to his eyes and fixed them on Anic. He could see the anger in the man's red face. As he screamed, spittle flew from his mouth, covering the man he was shouting at.

"All teams, go go go!" shouted Anderson, making the split second decision that this was his ideal opportunity to go in. Whilst Anic was angry and distracted. Anderson presumed Anic had just had a call from Wainwright telling him he wasn't going to turn up with the drugs after all. A situation which suited Anderson nicely.

He stayed behind the cars of the armed officers that burst into the yard and screeched to a halt. As the police emerged from their cars, their shouted orders caught all the men by surprise, causing confusion in Anic's ranks. Anderson wasn't surprised by their reaction. The cacophony of voices all shouting, "Armed police!" "Stand still!" "Do not move!" "Hands on your head!" "Drop your weapon!" over and over again was frightening and disorienting. Although he had expected the melee, even Anderson was rather overwhelmed with the noise and confusion it provoked.

The dark blue uniforms of the officers and the stomping of their high booted feet gave the impression of a marauding Army of beetles, swarming all over the unit and the car park. He watched as a line of them forced their way into the unit itself, emerging a few moments later with three men, all disarmed and with their hands on their heads.

Not being armed himself, Anderson had to wait until everyone had been contained before emerging from behind the safety of a police car. He strode over to Josip Anic and stood just that bit too close to the man, hoping to unsettle Anic further by invading his personal space.

"Good morning, Josip. Remember me?"

"Anderson, what the hell do you want?" As he spat the words out it was clear Anic's anger hadn't subsided. Well it wouldn't have done, though Anderson wryly to himself. The raid would have just wound him up even tighter.

"Just wondering who you were waiting for," Anderson said.

"Waiting for? I've no idea what you're talking about." Anic's face was still flushed red.

"Oh, I thought you were waiting for Bob Wainwright and his heroin from Afghanistan."

Anderson saw Anic's body still as he digested that

piece of information. Then his face went blank. "No comment," was all he said with a small upward nod of his head.

"Really?" asked Anderson. "Then what is all this for?" and at his nod a member of the response team threw a bag full of money on the floor between the two men. "I bet this lot is payment for the drugs. All ready and waiting for Wainwright, eh?"

"No comment."

"Whatever," Anderson swept Anic's words away with his hand and then cleared his throat, stood up straight, brushed down his tweed jacket and looking into Anic's eyes said, "Josip Anic I am arresting you for conspiracy to purchase and distribute Class A drugs. Anything you say…"

As Anderson finished the official wording of the Police Caution, Anic didn't slump under the weight of the words as Anderson had expected, but shook himself free of the two officers detaining him.

Flexing his muscled arms he spat, "I said no comment, you bastard." The accompanying piercing stare would have frightened a lesser police officer, but Anderson had too many years service under his belt and he merely laughed in the gangster's face.

The Hand Over

Kerry was getting a bit fed of up waiting. She fidgeted uncontrollably. Firstly patting Tyler's back, then rubbing it, then rocking her, then smoothing down her hair. Finally she spoke. "Are you sure they'll be here soon?" she asked Padre Symmonds.

"Oh, very sure. Don't worry, Kerry."

"It's just I can't believe it's taking them so long. Don't they want Tyler back?"

"I know that they very much want Tyler back, Kerry."

"Well, I hope they do. And I hope they are ready to mend their ways."

"Mend their ways? Whatever do you mean?"

"Well," Kerry looked around to make sure no one else was there and listening to their conversation, "I suppose I might as well tell you now. Then you can speak to them. The voice of authority as it were. Tell them."

The Padre moved from behind his desk and sat on the easy chair opposite her. "Okay, I'm listening," he said and leaned towards her as if he was slightly deaf and wanted to make sure he caught all her words.

"What do you want me to tell them?"

"I don't know if you know, but they're not very good parents." She had leaned forward as she spoke the words and then sat up straight, a note of triumph in her voice and nodded to the Padre. "I know Julie from the Mother and Baby Group and she was always saying that her husband Bob was never at home. Never seemed to do much around the house. Never seemed to have any time for Tyler."

She could see the Padre was listening closely to her words, so she decided to continue. "He used to shout a lot, apparently. Shouted at her. Shouted at the baby. Got upset and angry when Julie couldn't keep Tyler quiet. I ask you, what sort of father is that?"

That had set the Padre straight. She could see it. Disbelief that parents could act like that was etched on his face. It gave her the impetus she needed to continue.

"And Julie wasn't much better, you know. I ask you, leaving the baby outside a shop while she went to get pasties for her husband's lunch. I would have told him to get his own lunch as I was with the baby." She nodded in agreement with her words and smiled a smug smile. "Honestly, why couldn't she put the baby first? That's what a mother has to do, you know. Put her baby first. Protect her above anything and anyone else."

That made her think of Molly and her eyes filled with tears. "I wasn't given the chance to do that. To protect Molly as she grew up. A chance to show her how much I loved her by making her the centre of my world."

She managed to sniff back the tears. For this was no time for looking back at her own life. It was all about looking forward and Tyler's life. "That's what Julie has to do now," she said. "You see that don't you?"

It would appear the Padre did, for he nodded his head in agreement.

"Um," he said, "sorry Kerry, but who is Molly?"

"Why my own lovely baby," Kerry said thinking the man was going a bit mad. It wasn't that difficult to understand, surely. "Don't you remember? She died in the night so I left her here so you could look after her." Kerry couldn't stop her tears. They seemed to have a life of their own, falling out of her eyes without restraint and falling onto the top of Tyler's head. "You did look after her didn't you? You must have done. Tell me you have!"

"Of course I did, Kerry."

"Did you bury her? Laid her to rest here at the church?" Kerry bawled and wrapped her arms around Tyler, trying to get some comfort from cuddling the child that she would soon have to give back.

"Yes, I gave her a proper funeral and burial, Kerry. It's alright, there's no need to get so upset."

The Padre's words were soothing and Kerry tried to control her emotions by remembering why she was here.

"But I didn't know her name, so I haven't done a headstone yet," the Padre continued.

"Oh." Kerry cocked her head on one side, trying to remember what she did all those weeks ago. She was still crying, but had managed to calm her breathing and the sobs were subsiding.

"You're right. I should have left a letter or something shouldn't I? Then you would have known her name was Molly." She swiped away the tears from her cheeks using the sleeve of her coat.

"Not to worry, I know now," replied the Padre.

"Would you like to see where she's buried?"

"Oh, yes please. That would be lovely."

The Padre went to get out of his chair.

"Oh, not yet," Kerry shouted at him. "We can't go yet. We've got to wait for Julie and Bob. We'll go afterwards. And don't forget you have to explain to them what bad parents they used to be so they'll understand what they've done wrong. They must promise you that they'll try to be better parents. Promise to put the baby first in future."

"Yes, of course," the Padre agreed and sat back in his chair. "More coffee?"

Kerry nodded and watched Padre Symmonds as he fussed over his coffee pot. What a silly man he was, she thought. Thinking I would go to see Molly before I've sorted Tyler out. That's the trouble with men. They never think rationally when it comes to babies. She did hope he'd get her message across to the Wainwrights. Make them understand they had to put Tyler first. She stroked the baby's back again and murmured to her, telling her mummy would be here soon and then she could go home.

She was interrupted by a noise outside the Padre's office. He looked up from the coffee pot and said, "Just stay there a minute, Kerry. It sounds like Bob and Julie are here."

Kerry breathed deeply several times. To make sure she was ready to do this. To hand Tyler back to her parents. As Julie came into the room, Kerry stood and faced her.

"Hello, Julie," Kerry said, wrapping her arms protectively around Tyler in the carrier. "How lovely to see you again. Why don't you sit down? I'm sure the Padre will make you a cup of coffee. It's really rather good. Does Bob want one as well?" Kerry turned and looked at Bob Wainwright.

His face was inscrutable. Typical soldier, thought Kerry. Won't show his emotions. Won't give away how he's feeling. She still wasn't sure about him. Wasn't sure that he was capable of being a good father. But she had to trust the Padre, she supposed.

"I, don't, um," Julie stammered a reply to the offer of coffee.

Kerry wondered why she looked so pale and skinny. "Have you been ill?" she asked her, worried now that Julie wasn't in any fit state to look after Tyler.

"Ill? No, no, just a bit…"

"Ah, I understand," nodded Kerry. "Just a bit worried about Tyler?"

"Yes, could I have her back now?" and Julie reached out her arms towards the baby.

"In a minute." Kerry took a step back from her. "The Padre has something to say to you and your husband first. Haven't you Padre?"

37

Julie Wainwright walked into the Padre's small office in the church with more than a bit of trepidation. She couldn't bring herself to believe that at last she would get Tyler back. But as she looked around and her gaze lit upon Kerry, she began to believe it may actually be true after all, for there was Kerry, large as life, with a baby in a carrier strapped to her chest.

Julie knew her appearance wasn't up to much. She had lost at least a stone in weight and her skin was in the most appalling condition with spots breaking out on her chin and worry lines that were probably permanent, carved into her forehead. But Kerry didn't look a picture herself. Her red spiralled curls were stuck out from her head like an incongruous afro. She had inexpertly applied green eye shadow and her lips were a garish slash of red that clashed with her ginger hair.

Kerry was sat in a comfortable chair, near the coffee pot and invited Julie to sit opposite her. She'd rather have her baby back than sit down, but did as she was asked, wondering how long this stupid charade was going to go on for. Then Kerry offered her coffee - just as if they'd been meeting at one another's houses, or at the mother and baby group. It was beyond belief! She shot a look at Bob. But he was of no help, for he had his soldier's face on as she called it. The one that said he was behind his barrier. Emotionless. Aloof. Oblivious to her distress.

Groping behind her, she managed to collapse into a chair before she fell over and mumbled something to the offer of coffee. But she did manage to find her voice and ask for her baby back. In response to that, Kerry told them the Padre had something to say to them first, so they all turned towards Padre Symmonds. They moved woodenly, as if they were puppets, unable to move voluntarily, only able to dance to Kerry's tune, for the mad woman held their strings.

To be truthful, Julie wasn't taking in any of the Padre's words. She vaguely heard him say something about parenting and not leaving the baby alone again. She managed to nod in what she hoped were the right places, for all she could do was stare at the baby in the carrier, who didn't seem to move much. Perhaps she was asleep? Concentrating on the bulky shape, she was sure she could see Tyler breathing. There was a slight movement of the chest up and down - wasn't there?

Then the baby cried. It was more like a whimper, really, but it startled them all and stopped Padre Symmonds' bumbling words about putting the baby first. Kerry looked down at the baby and replaced the dummy her mouth.

Julie heard the Padre say, "Don't you think you should hand Tyler back now, Kerry?"

Watching Kerry unbuckle the carrier, strap by strap, was agony. Julie wrung her hands together over and over again as she sat on the edge of her seat, poised to take Tyler once she was free. No one spoke. Julie looked up and saw that Sgt Major Crane had slipped silently into the room and joined them. She also caught sight of Kim Symmonds, who was standing in the doorway. Everyone was watching Kerry.

At last the straps were all undone and Kerry cradled the baby in her arms. She leaned down and kissed her cheek, then held her out to Julie.

With arms that didn't seem to belong to her, Julie reached out towards Tyler as she stood up. Kerry stood as well and at last put Tyler back into her mother's arms.

"Thank you so much, Kerry," the Padre said and immediately moved to stand between the two women. He was probably making sure Kerry couldn't grab her back, thought Julie as she adjusted the child in her arms to make sure she had a better hold on her.

"Why don't you go with my wife Kim?" the Padre asked Kerry. "She'll be happy to show you where Molly is buried."

Kerry must have agreed, but Julie wasn't taking any notice, just staring at the child in her arms. Tyler's hair was the right colour, but not quite the right style. Her cheeks were all red and rosy which was unusual for Tyler, who only got like that when she was screaming due to teething or colic. Julie could feel Tyler breathing, but no other part of her was moving. Not her head, her arms, nor her legs. She fell back into the chair she had just risen from and as she did she accidently brushed the baby's face. When she felt the cold porcelain underneath her fingers, she started to scream.

38

Crane had just managed to whisper to Kim, "Hand Kerry over to Billy and Sgt Jones. They're waiting in the body of the church," when all hell let loose.

Julie Wainwright started screaming and threw the baby away from her as though it were scorching her hands. He quickly shut the door behind Kim and Kerry, to stop them returning, as the child crashed onto the floor. When he looked back into the room, he saw Tyler lying on the carpet between the two chairs, splayed out on the bright rug.

Wainwright seemed paralysed, as did the Padre, for they were both stood there as if turned to stone by Medusa, staring down at Tyler. So it was Crane who took the few paces from the door to the sitting area. He squatted down to pick up the child, wondering why she hadn't cried as she hit the floor. And that's when he saw why she hadn't. That was when he saw the large crack in her face that ran from her chin up through her nose, travelling up over her forehead and disappearing into her hair. One of her eyes was missing, leaving a gaping hole where the organ should have been. The eyeball itself had rolled away and come to rest against the table leg. It was lying there, staring up at Crane.

He stood and backed away from the doll in horror. He realised what they hadn't seen before. That the baby Kerry had brought to be handed back to her parents, was nothing more than one of those reborn dolls. He turned to Julie, who was still screaming. He opened his mouth to try and comfort her, but he couldn't find the right words, couldn't find any words, and all that happened was that he opened and closed his mouth like a fish beached on the shore. Anyway words couldn't even begin to describe his own horror and confusion. Underneath that, he felt immense sadness for Julie Wainwright, who didn't know it yet, but had not only lost her child, but was about to lose her husband. Despite feeling completely inadequate, he realised he must do something, so he grabbed the screaming woman and pulled her close. At his touch, Julie began to calm down, collapsing against him, sobbing, so Crane took her weight and held her upright.

He looked across at the Padre who seemed to be recovering from the initial shock and at Crane's silent plea he walked forward, taking Julie and sitting her back down in the chair. The Padre indicated with his head that Bob Wainwright should come and comfort his wife.

Bob moved to squat by Julie's chair and clumsily put his arm around her. Looking at the two men standing above him he said, "Would someone please tell me what the hell is going on here?"

How on earth do I explain this one, thought Crane and took a moment to crystallise his thoughts before saying, "I'm so sorry, but it looks like Tyler is nothing more than a reborn doll."

"A what?" the Padre asked.

"A doll?" Wainwright said at the same time.

"A reborn doll," said Crane. "It's a doll that is made to look as human as possible. They can be battery powered to give the impression of breathing, they can also have a pre-recorded chip inside them so they cry and some even move their hands to grab your finger," he explained.

"That's gross," said Wainwright. "But if this is a doll, then where the hell is Tyler?"

Crane didn't want to answer that question, but it looked like Bob got the general idea from his silence.

"Jesus Christ," Wainwright said and turned once again to his wife.

Kim led Kerry away from the closed office door which had subdued the noise of Julie Wainwright's screams.

"Is Julie alright?" Kerry asked her, trying to turn and go back into the Padre's office.

Kim held her tightly by the elbow and kept moving away from the door. "Yes, I'm sure Julie's just fine. Anyway there are three men in there to help her if she needs it."

"Only, it's just that she may be a bit startled when she sees Tyler."

Kim stopped walking. "Why would she be startled, Kerry? What's wrong with Tyler?"

"Oh, nothing's wrong with her, it's just that she's been reborn."

"Reborn?" Kim started marching Kerry through the corridor towards the body of the church again, eager to get rid of this mad woman into the custody of Billy and Jones. "What does reborn mean?"

"Well, because Tyler died, I had to replace her with a reborn. You know what I mean, don't you? You buy them off the internet."

"Internet?" asked Kim weakly, unable to stop a look of abject horror crossing her face.

"Yes, some of the sites are ever so good. Anyways I trawled through them all until I found Tyler. I knew she'd be waiting for me somewhere on there. I bet you're impressed that I found her amongst all those dolls, aren't you?"

Kerry's proud smile was more than Kim could bear.

"Julie will be fine about it in the end. Just you see," Kerry prattled on. "Because Tyler's much better behaved now you know. She breathes and cries a bit and sucks her dummy. But she doesn't scream anymore, or throw up her dinner, or crawl all over the flat and get under my feet. Yes, I'm sure Julie will be happier with the reborn Tyler than with the other one."

Kerry smiled happily at Billy and Jones as they approached them and said, "Are you taking me to see Molly's grave now? The Padre said someone would."

"Yes, that's right, love," Jones agreed, as if he understood what Kerry was talking about. "Just come with us, we'll go in the car as it's quite a way down to the cemetery."

As Jones turned away, leading Kerry out of the church, Kim told Billy the horrendous news.

"So what happens now?" Wainwright asked Crane.

"The Padre is ringing for a doctor, for your wife. Once he's been I'll get him and Kim to take her home and make sure someone stays with her. Does she have a particular friend?"

"Well I suppose if anyone its Linda from next door. She's probably your best bet. Can't stand the woman myself, but Julie seems to get on with her right enough," Wainwright shrugged his shoulders.

"As for you," Crane said, "you're coming back with me to Provost Barracks."

Bob nodded. "I rather thought I was."

Julie stirred in her chair. "Provost Barracks? Who's going to Provost Barracks?"

"Your husband is, I'm afraid, Julie."

"Why," she struggled to stand up. "Does he have to make a statement or something?"

"Yes, he needs to make a statement."

She turned to Bob, "You'll come back home afterwards, though, won't you? Don't leave me alone tonight, Bob."

"I'm afraid Bob won't be coming home tonight, Julie," Crane said. "In fact he won't be going anywhere for quite a few years, I'd say."

"You're not? Years? Bob?"

Bob Wainwright swallowed, but couldn't seem to get the words out, so Crane said them for him. "Because he's been smuggling, Julie. Working with someone in Afghanistan. Smuggling drugs that arrived a couple of weeks ago, but he hasn't had chance to pass them along yet, because of the incident with Tyler."

"Oh, so you know about that then," she said flatly.

"We'll need to interview you as well, but that can wait until tomorrow."

Turning to Wainwright, he arrested and cautioned him, whilst Julie stood looking on, alternating her gaze between the broken doll on the floor that had been her daughter and the broken man in front of her that had been her husband.

After Crane finished speaking she asked her husband, "Why did you do it, Bob? Why did you betray the Army you love by using it to smuggle heroin?"

Crane wasn't surprised when Bob said, "I've never felt that way about the Army, you silly cow. I just faked it. The higher up the ranks I went the more opportunities for smuggling and selling stuff on the black market presented themselves. That what I liked about the Army."

"But I believed in it, Bob, believed in the honour and the way of life and the regiment - all of it!"

He laughed and replied, "Well more fool you, then," as Crane handcuffed him and led him away. As they walked through the corridor he could hear Julie Wainwright shouting, "Come back! You heartless bastard, Crane! How can you arrest my husband and take him away when I've just found out Tyler is dead!"

As her screams echoed around the vaulted ceiling and bounced off the cold hard stone, Crane hoped the doctor would arrive soon.

39

Crane and Anderson stood outside the front door of Kerry's flat.

"Ready?" Anderson asked Crane.

"Not really. But we'd better get on with it."

Anderson pulled Kerry's keys out of his pocket and worked the mostly likely key into the lock. The lock clicked open as he turned the key and he then pushed the door open with his gloved hand.

"So, you think Tyler could be in the flat?"

"I hope so," Anderson replied. "We've not had any other reports of a very young child being left anywhere in the region, dead or alive."

Crane followed the policeman into the flat, their overshoes rustling against the meagre carpet. "You've not been here before, have you?" Crane asked him.

"No." Looking around Anderson then said, "It doesn't look like I've missed much. Not exactly out of House and Homes is it?"

The two men looked around the sad living space. The tatty furniture matched the tatty carpets. The black smudged damp walls were doing a good job of repelling the wallpaper. It was tidy enough, but because of the age of the furniture and bad décor, it was one of those places that would always look dirty. There were very few places in the small room that a body could have been hidden in, but they looked anyway.

"It doesn't smell as though there's a body in the apartment," Crane said. At Anderson's glare he finished, "Sorry, but there would be a strong smell of decomposition."

"Yes, I know. Let's try the kitchen. The fridge or something."

Crane wasn't enjoying this any more than Anderson was. The place was giving him the creeps. He followed Anderson into the small kitchen, made smaller by the chest freezer poking out of the small utility area. Both men looked at it.

"Well?" Crane asked.

"I think so, don't you?"

At Crane's nod, Anderson walked over and lifted the lid. Crane followed and looked over Anderson's shoulder. But he knew Tyler was in there before he saw the body, for he had seen the slump of Anderson's shoulders and the bowing of his head.

Tyler was lying on top of the bags of vegetables, in one of the baskets. Frozen solid. Wrapped in an icy blanket. The most poignant thing, Crane thought, was the frost on her eye lashes.

They were interrupted by banging on the front door.

"That'll be Scene of Crime," Anderson said and turned away to let them in. Crane stood looking at the tiny body for a few more moments. His thoughts were a maelstrom. Thoughts of Kerry, who seemed to have been spiralling into madness ever since her husband was killed and who had now been Sectioned under The Mental Health Act and was being looked after in hospital. He thought about Julie who had lost her daughter and husband, just as Kerry had, but under very different circumstances. In the mix were the deaths of two innocent children. Molly from cot death and Tyler from what? Well the post mortem would answer that question. Would determine if they would charge Kerry with murder, or just abduction.

As for Wainwright, he would be charged with smuggling Class A drugs at the very least and Crane was sure he could add a few more charges of his own to the list. Josip Anic would be charged with whatever Anderson could dream up and then make stick. He would have to talk to Derek about Julie Wainwright. They would have to decide if they would charge her with perverting the cause of justice, for not telling them about the drugs, which she clearly knew Bob had stored in their garage.

"Ready to go, Crane?" Anderson called from the doorway. "The techies need us to vacate so they can get on with collecting their forensic evidence."

Crane turned to face his friend. "Yes," he nodded. "I need to get out of here."

As they walked out onto the balcony, Crane took a deep breath of air, but then wished he hadn't as the pungent smell of urine was pulled into his lungs, making him cough.

"At least Julie Wainwright will have a child to bury," he said to Anderson when he recovered.

"Once everything's sorted out."

"Yes, once everything's sorted out," Crane agreed.

As they walked away Anderson asked, "Did you notice a smell in the living room as we walked back through it just now."

"A smell? The only thing I can smell is the stench of

pee on this balcony. Is that what you mean?"

"No, that's not it. Does Kerry smoke, do you know?"

"No, I don't think so. Why?"

"Because I'm sure I got a whiff of smoke as I passed the armchair."

40

"So what's with these reborn dolls?" Draper asked Crane as they finished their debriefing. "They're not something I've come across before."

"Me neither, boss," said Crane. "They're a bit bloody creepy I can tell you."

"You're right there. But there must be some sort of physiological reason for someone like Kerry to use them."

Crane settled himself more comfortably in his chair opposite Draper's desk. "From what I can understand, the reality is that people often face sorrowful issues in their lives. In many cases, they use denial to cope with that loss and the resulting anxiety. And some are unfortunate enough to have lost a child - one of the most devastating things that can happen in anyone's life. It's a case of what the mind does when faced with such a void."

"Oh, you mean Kerry refused to accept that her daughter was dead?"

"Something along those lines, boss. Denial is one of the most prominent defence mechanisms. It's not that most of these doll-owners think the doll is a real baby, but it affords them moments when they are comforted and can pretend to themselves and to the world, that they do have a real baby. According to the doctors, it provides moments of relief and reprieve, when they can escape the stark reality of their loss. An opportunity for them to have those familiar feelings of cuddling a baby, cooing over it, and all those other nice moments, that temporarily undo the harsh reality. We think Kerry grew too attached to her doll babies, indicating her grief was not actually getting resolved. One of the risks of having this kind of doll is that it can become too literal, too concrete to the women. That's when we think Kerry started to think the dolls were real.

"Didn't she keep saying that the dolls were better than the real babies?"

"Yes. She told Kim she thought Julie would prefer the new reborn Tyler, for unlike a real baby, a lifelike doll comes with no real-world mess. No nappies, no smells, no feeding, no crying. These babies, unlike real ones, don't grow up into toddlers. And as soon as the child becomes a toddler, there's a whole different dynamic. A creature growing, changing and moving toward independence. It will, clearly, need the mother less and less. Intertwined with a doll baby is the knowledge it will never grow up, never leave you, never disappoint you, never say 'I hate you!'"

"Jesus Christ!" said Draper. After a moment's thought he said, "I suppose that if a woman walks around with a baby - or a doll that looks like a baby - everyone stops to admire it. So having one produces positive attention, like when you are dressed up and people admire you. For a woman who is struggling to feel good about herself, the baby provides reassurances. Especially for a woman in Kerry's position, who had lost not only her husband, but her child. I guess for a confused and bruised mind, she saw the doll as a way back into the normal world."

"That's right, boss. There are many ways a person can cope with loss, sadness and anxiety, and these reborn dolls offer one solution. Unfortunately Kerry's relationship with the reborn dolls grew into an unreasonable obsession.

"I guess she's staying in hospital?"

"Yes, mental health treatment is absolutely necessary, the doctors have said. Kerry's depression spiralled into a dependency on nurturing something that's not living. She's going to need years of treatment to help her out of the obsession she's become buried in."

41

The Padre put his hand on his coffee mug and lifted it to his lips without looking at it. He realised too late, as he went to take a sip, that it was cold. Spluttering and grimacing, he looked away from the computer screen that he had been transfixed on, where he had been reviewing his report on the welfare case of Bob and Julie Wainwright.

He put his mug down with a sigh and wiped his lips with a tissue grabbed from the box on his desk. The sigh was for many things, for he wasn't feeling at his most upbeat that morning. Writing the report had brought back all the horrors of his time with the Wainwrights whilst everyone was looking for their baby. And then the time he spent with Kerry in his office at the church, while they were waiting for the Wainwrights to come and collect baby Tyler.

He'd never encountered someone with such a clear severe mental problem before and his heart went out to Kerry as much as Julie Wainwright. However, he wasn't sure he had much sympathy for Bob Wainwright, who was now incarcerated in the military prison at Colchester.

He prised himself from his comfy leather chair to go and get some more coffee, when Kim walked in, a steaming mug in her hand.

"Thought you might need more caffeine," she said. "You know, to help with writing the report."

Francis sat back down and gratefully took the coffee from Kim.

"How's it going? Or do you want to be left alone?"

"Not well and no I don't," he said answering her two questions. "Can you sit for a minute?"

Kim nodded and sat opposite him, the large desk somehow symbolising the yawning gap between then, not just physically, but also mentally and Francis was immediately aware of his other problem. Kim.

"It's just that it's brought it all back, writing this report," he said.

"I know, it must be awful for you to have to re-live it again," she said, smiling, but in sympathy more than anything.

"It's, um, not just them. Kerry, Tyler, Julie and Bob," he indicated his screen. "It's, um, you, or should I say, us, as well."

"What?" Kim's surprise seemed genuine. "Francis, what on earth are you talking about?"

"Well, you know that I wondered if being involved with the investigation would make you miss being in the Branch. Make you homesick for the office, somehow."

"Yes, I remember you asking."

"And I remember you not replying."

Kim sat there, looking at him coolly. Her expression wasn't uncompassionate, but she was, well, just there. Not fidgeting or looking bored. Just waiting, with interest, for him to speak again."

"See, you're doing it now," he said.

She smiled. "Doing what?"

"Not answering the question and waiting to hear what I say next. It's not a bad thing, don't get me wrong. It's just this knack you have. You're a very good listener."

"Sorry, I don't mean to upset you," she said. "I'm just not sure what you think is wrong."

Francis decided to go for it. After all, he had nothing to lose. So he took a deep breath and said, "I think you're bored. Or you're going to get bored. It was fine when you were needed to help support Julie Wainwright and when you were helping Crane. But now that's all over and I'm just worried that you won't know what to do with yourself and you'll begin to wish you'd never married me and…" His voice trailed away.

This was much harder, he decided, talking about feelings. He was too used to listening to others as they told him what they were feeling.

Kim stayed quiet. No doubt trying to work out how to tell him she wasn't happy, was Francis' first thought. He grabbed his coffee and took a drink, to try and swallow his fear.

"You're right," she said eventually.

Francis put down his coffee and closed his eyes. Here it comes, he thought.

"I do need something to do. I need to find a role for myself. But within our life, Francis." Kim leaned towards him and took his hands which were clasped together, resting on his desk. "I really enjoyed helping you with supporting the Wainwrights. Far more than I did with assisting Sgt Major Crane."

That made him sit up and take notice. "Really?"

"Really," she agreed. "I've been thinking about it

and thinking about it until at times I've been going a bit nuts. But I think I've got it worked out now."

She let go of his hands and took a gulp of his coffee. Putting it down, she looked at him and said, "I want to train as a counsellor."

"Thank goodness for that," Francis said and sent a silent thank you arrow prayer to God for his intervention. "I was so afraid…"

She smiled. "I know. I'm sorry. Maybe I should have talked to you sooner, but I just wanted to get it all straight in my mind. See, if I train as a counsellor, I could be an asset to you, as well as just your wife. I could step in when you're away, and do something really worthwhile to help you." Kim was becoming animated and had a wide grin on her face. "I don't think I want to set up my own practice, but I wouldn't mind working at a charity, for abused women, for instance. I don't know, something like that, anyway. But whatever I do, first I want to train. Be a professional,, not just your wife who happens to be a good listener."

"What do you have to do to be qualified?"

"Well, two years to start with, college, course work and stuff and practised supervision. But if I want to specialise in abuse or addiction, then there'd be another year so I could get an Advanced Diploma. Of course, I'd have to spend a lot of a time on that, and I won't necessarily be much help to you while I'm doing it. And then of course there's the tuition fees. So, um, what do you think? Are you happy with that? Can you let me do my own thing? I hope you don't think I'm letting you down."

"Kim, you silly woman. Of course you're not letting me down. I'd be happy to support you in whatever you want to do. And I think being a counsellor would suit you to a 't'. Where can you go to train? Have you got any information from local colleges?"

"Yes, I printed some prospectuses off the internet. I'll show you later, when you're not busy."

"Kim, I'm never too busy for you. Go and get them, let's have a look at them together."

As Kim veritably skipped out of the room, Francis sunk back in his chair and vowed never to doubt his beautiful wife's commitment to their marriage, or love for him, ever again.

42

Alan sat in his armchair, in the still of the empty room, wondering what had happened to his wife. He'd been a bit perturbed over the past few days, what with all those people coming and going in and out of the flat. Every time he tried to check up on Kerry, to see if she was home yet, there would be someone else in the flat and he'd have to quickly disappear. But now, for the first time, everyone had left and he was alone.

He looked around and saw that every surface was covered in a black powder that he guessed was that finger print stuff. Although whose finger prints they were checking for he couldn't imagine. Kerry never had any visitors. Apart from those two blokes from the Branch. He'd forgotten about them.

He sat and listened, hoping to hear something. A rustle of clothes, a cough, a snore. Anything. But there wasn't a sound. Kerry wasn't there.

He was pretty sure she wasn't dead, otherwise she'd be with him already, he reasoned. He thought back to the last time he saw her. She'd gone to give Tyler back. Where was she going? Oh yes, the Garrison Church. He remembered their conversation now. The one where they'd debated whether or not the Wainwright's were good enough parents. Talked about whether or not they'd deserved to have their baby back.

But as that was several days ago and she'd not come back since, it was clear to him that something had gone wrong. He wondered where she might be. With the Padre? With the Wainwrights? Oh hell. He suddenly realised, she might have been arrested. If that was the case, she could be at a police station, answering questions, or even in jail.

Fighting his rising panic, he reasoned he must find her and support her. She was in this position because of him. If he hadn't been blown up everything would be alright. So really, all of it was his fault. He couldn't just sit in his armchair and wait, so he decided he must start looking for her right away. He'd try the Garrison Church, first. He hoped she wasn't with the Wainwrights, because he didn't know where they lived.

He looked across at the two Mollies. One was in her high chair and the other in the playpen. They looked as beautiful as the day they'd arrived. As he watched them he smiled, for he loved them as much as he'd loved the real Molly. They were his children now and it was up to him to look after them.

Turning slightly in his chair, he called out to them. Once he had their attention, he promised them he'd be back soon. He was just going to find Mummy, he said. He reminded them that they had to be good little girls and behave while he was away.

Then he shimmered and gradually faded away. Leaving behind just a small wisp of grey smoke.

Keep reading for a preview of Hijack

Hijack

Terrified and imprisoned on a train on a viaduct with a deathly 100' drop. Do the hostages have what it takes to stay alive? Or will the terrorists win?

When a mysterious group of cyclists board a train, one of them pulls the emergency cord and the train grinds to a halt on the Ribblehead Viaduct, a 100ft high structure with a deathly fall. The six hijackers are armed with guns and bombs and are prepared to do anything, to achieve their aims, even if it results in the death of innocent people.

Hijack is the sixth in the Sgt Major Crane crime thriller series.

> 'More tears are shed over answered prayers, than unanswered ones.'
> Truman Capote

Prologue

**Bagram Detention Centre
Afghanistan**

The young man swung from a rope tied around his hands and attached to a metal hook in the ceiling. He'd been up there for five hours. Luckily he'd died after three. His poor tortured and abused body no longer able to take the punishment meted out by the soldiers.

The naked light bulb in the cell was burning, as it had done since the boy's arrival at the detention centre several months earlier, harshly illuminating the bare concrete walls, ceiling and floor. There had been no respite from the light. Nor from the shouting of the soldiers as they tortured other prisoners in the block.

Although he had been young and strong when grabbed from the garage by the coalition forces, where he was working on a Land Rover that refused to start, it hadn't saved him. For some reason the soldiers seemed to think he was part of an illegal militia, not a simple motor mechanic. No matter what he'd said, how long and hard he'd screamed or whimpered and cried, they'd ignored his distress and continued with the beatings and interrogations.

Being fed on the occasional chunk of bread and jug

of water pushed contemptuously into his cell, had meant his body soon turned against him, burning up fat and muscle in the absence of the fuel it needed to survive. Daily and nightly attacks from fists, batons and worse, had worn out his wasted body, until one by one his internal organs shut down.

The last to go was his heart. As it beat its final tattoo the boy's thoughts were for his family. Did they know where he was? Would they be told he'd died? Would his brother, Kourash, thousands of miles away in England hear of his fate?

With his last breath he whispered his father's name...

Day One

09:55 hours

He'd known there was something wrong the minute he saw them through the window. The innocuous group of cyclists waiting to board the train at Dent railway station. It wasn't because they were sweating, although the day was sunny but cold. It wasn't even that they were looking nervously around, their eyes always going back to the tallest young man in the middle of their huddled group, as if seeking reassurance. Nor the fact that as soon as the train juddered to a stop at the platform they immediately split up, boarding the train in two groups. One group to each of the two carriages, instead of staying together. It wasn't those things individually. But put them together? Well that was a cause for concern.

As this was happening, Sgt Billy Williams was on the phone to his boss, Sgt Major Crane. Billy had rung him to confirm he'd be at Aldershot Garrison later that day, reporting back to Provost Barracks, the home of the Special Investigations Branch of the Royal Military Police. Billy was taking the scenic train route, from Carlisle to Settle, on the return journey from his parent's house in Carlisle, where he'd spent the weekend.

Billy watched with interest the young men who boarded the carriage. One boy took off the scarf he was wearing around his neck, revealing two sturdy bicycle chains with locks on. He took them from around his neck and passed one to his fellow traveller. The young man tethered his bike to the pole by the carriage entrance, as did his companion. Why would you chain your bike to the pole if you were staying in the carriage, Billy wondered? Were they that distrustful of people? Or was there an ulterior motive? Once the bikes were chained up, the two young men seemed unable to keep still. Hands wringing. Brows sweating. Teeth chewing lips. It made Billy nervous just watching them. With a suspicious frown, he looked out of the window. The train was approaching the Ribble Viaduct, a 100 foot high structure with 24 arches. A remote construction set high up on the Yorkshire Dales and now a popular tourist attraction. The viaduct had been built in the 1800's by hundreds of Irish navvies who lived and worked on the construction site. But there were no shanty towns still standing. All trace of the workers had been wiped from the face of the barren earth and the Dales returned to their majestic, isolated, glory.

As one of the cyclists moved to stand close to the emergency stop cord, Billy said into his mobile phone, 'Boss, I think there's a problem with the Carlisle to Settle train.' He was going to add - I think the shit's just about to hit the fan - when it well and truly did. The cyclist reached for the emergency cord and yanked it.

So with the cool calm reactions ingrained in him from his military training, Billy said instead, 'Possible hijack situation. The train's stopping in the middle of the Ribble Viaduct. Estimate at least six hijackers, cyclists who boarded the train at Dent. Will report back when I know more.'

But his calm, quick reactions didn't stop him feeling apprehensive. Fear wriggled like a worm through his veins. A purveyor of bad news. With worse to come, no doubt.

Billy had instinctively risen from his seat during the conversation and holding the seat backs, using them to keep his balance during the sharp reduction in the speed of the train, he made his way to the toilet. He was talking to Crane via the hands-free mobile phone cord that ran from his ear to his phone, which was hidden from view in the pocket of his brown leather jacket.

With the door closed, the smell of the chemical toilet was strong in the small space and he breathed through his mouth in an effort to minimise it. Cutting the call and then turning off the volume on his mobile, he looked around the tiny cubicle. All the surfaces were stainless steel and the small space seemed coffin-like and claustrophobic. The walls were pre-fabricated and moulded, with no cracks or gaps in them that he could utilise. Bugger. He needed a hiding place and he needed it now. There would only be a few moment's grace before he was found. Then he spotted a small cupboard built into the wall underneath the sink. Squatting down and grasping the handle, Billy was relieved to find the cupboard unlocked. He popped his phone inside and plugged the cord, which was still dangling from his ear, into his iPod instead. Straightening up he pushed open the door and backed out of the toilet. Slap bang into the barrel of a revolver. A small smile played across Billy's lips. The game was on.

Meet the Author

I do hope you've enjoyed Regenerate. If so, perhaps you would be kind enough to post a review on Amazon. Reviews really do make all the difference to authors and it is great to get feedback from you, the reader.

If this is the first of my novels you've read, you may be interested in the other Sgt Major Crane books, following Tom Crane and DI Anderson as they take on the worst crimes committed in and around Aldershot Garrison. In order, they are: Steps to Heaven, 40 Days 40 Nights, Honour Bound, Cordon of Lies, Regenerate, Hijack, Glass Cutter and Solid Proof.

Crane and Anderson then solve more crimes in Death Rites, Death Elements, Death Call and A Grave Death.

Past Judgment is a spin-off from the Sgt Major Crane novels and features Emma Harrison from Hijack and Sgt Billy Williams of the Special Investigations Branch of the Royal Military Police.

All my books are available on Amazon.

Printed in Great Britain
by Amazon